the Blue Jay

MICHELLE SCHLICHER

Published by Michelle Schlicher
ISBN: 978-0-9965750-0-3

Copyright © Michelle Schlicher, 2015

That's Life
Words and Music by Dean Kay and Kelly Gordon
Copyright (c) 1964, 1966 UNIVERSAL - POLYGRAM INTERNATIONAL PUBLISHING, INC.
Copyright Renewed
All Rights Reserved Used by Permission
Reprinted by Permission of Hal Leonard Corporation

Cover design by Hanna Piepel
Layout by Guido Henkel

This is a work of fiction. Names, characters, businesses, places, events and incidents are either the products of the author's imagination or used in a fictitious manner. Any resemblance to actual persons, living or dead, or actual events is purely coincidental.

All rights reserved. Except as permitted under the U.S. Copyright Act of 1976, no part of this publication may be reproduced, distributed or transmitted in any form or by any means, or stored in a database or retrieval system, without the prior written permission of the publisher.

Printed in the U.S.A.

*For my daughters,
Sawyer and Sullivan*

*and for Trisha,
who inspired this story*

"A jay will lie, a jay will steal, a jay will deceive, a jay will betray; and four times out of five, a jay will go back on his solemnest promise. The sacredness of an obligation is a thing which you can't cram into no bluejay's head."

— *Mark Twain, What Stumped the Bluejays*

PROLOGUE

FOUR WORDS.

That was all it took to break Josie McCray's heart.

Josie, just eight years old at the time, woke up earlier than usual that morning. She padded over to her bedroom window, her pink nightgown too airy for this time of year but the fuzzy socks soft against her feet keeping her from getting too chilled. She gazed out at the giant snowflakes falling from the still dark sky. They moved so gracefully that Josie was reminded of the dancers in her favorite ballet, *The Nutcracker,* as they performed the Waltz of the Snowflakes. The snow must have been falling all night—it covered the entire yard, and from the window Josie could see her dad's copper bird feeder hanging from the old oak tree. The top was weighed down by a small mound of snow, but if you looked closely you could see it slowly swaying back and forth.

Thinking she was the only one awake in the house, she quietly pulled on a pair of sweatpants and tied her blonde curls into a low ponytail. As she stepped into the hallway, she paused, listening for the sound of her father's snoring. When she heard the familiar sound, she held onto the rail and crept down the wooden staircase. She was just about to the bottom when she tripped over her thick socks, falling the rest of the way and stubbing her toe on the last step.

The Blue Jay

"Ouch!" Josie said under her breath, catching herself from crying out at the pain.

She rubbed her big toe between her fingers, willing the hurt away, before remembering her original mission. Taking a deep breath, she continued through the house to the front door where she quickly put on her stocking cap. It was one of those hand-knit hats with the ball on top that always prompted comments like "Isn't that just precious?!" or "Haveyouever-seenanythingsocuteinyourlife?!" from the adults, like strangers in the checkout line at the grocery store and other parents watching their kids play at the park. Josie brushed a loose curl out of her face and tucked it up into the cap. She grabbed her coat and boots, pulling them on one at a time, all the while doing her best not to make a sound.

Once outside, she stood at the edge of the porch. The snow fell harder now and the wind invaded her eyes, causing them to water from the blast of cold that jolted her when she'd stepped out onto the porch. But Josie wasn't about to go back inside. She looked around at the winter wonderland that had, it seemed, magically appeared overnight. Had she ever seen anything so beautiful in her short life?

She stuck out her tongue to catch a falling snowflake, just the way she and Mia had done last winter. That was during the coldest winter Montpier had seen since the 60s—at least according to her father. Mia Shoning was four years older and lived in the bright yellow house next door. The girls became fast friends when Josie's family had moved to town a few years before. Unlike Josie, who was an only child, Mia's family was large. She was the last of six, which may have been why Mia was drawn to her in the first place. She would never have a younger sibling, and Josie had looked like a fine substitute for the relationship she thought she was missing out on.

As the snow fell, Josie peered into the darkness of the street. She pictured her neighbors all still warm in their beds, cherishing the last few moments of warmth before their morning routines began. A light went on in a bedroom across the street at Mr. DeWaay's, and she thought she heard a dog barking somewhere. She was listening for the sound again when she saw the headlights of a car turn onto the street.

Josie put her head back again and opened her mouth, catching another snowflake and savoring the sensation of the wetness on her tongue. She could have stayed like that a long time if she hadn't been distracted by those blaring headlights. Turning toward the car, Josie squinted through the snow, waiting for it to pass. It didn't, and instead came to a stop in front of their house. She stared, through the falling snow, trying to see the figure in the driver's seat.

Moments later, the sound of the front door opening and closing behind her cut short her examination of the car and its unknown driver. Josie turned to see her mother standing behind her, fully dressed and made up. She was holding the blue suitcase that Josie and her father had picked out for her as a Christmas gift just a few months before.

"Mama?"

Her mother didn't respond. Instead, she reached up and wiped a rogue snowflake from her face. As she glided past a stunned Josie, she smiled at the stranger in the car. Was he waiting for her? Josie wondered.

"Mama?" Josie said again, her voice breathless in the crisp winter air. "Where are you going?"

Josie felt her legs move beneath her. Her mother had reached the car and opened the door to the backseat when Josie caught up to her. She set the blue suitcase down inside. Josie shivered and pulled her hat down further on her head. The woman in front of her looked unfamiliar. It was scary to see her own mother looking like that—like a complete stranger. There was nothing physically different about her, but somehow, it wasn't her. Josie could see the driver now, his black mustache and wild eyes. She didn't recognize him, which frightened her even more.

"Mama!" she gasped, grabbing for her mother's arm.

Her mother finally turned, as if hearing her for the first time, and their eyes met. Later, she would see those eyes while she

The Blue Jay

slept, startling her from her dreams. They were the eyes of a newborn baby who couldn't yet see clearly, forcing the infant to use its other senses to determine the people and things around him. Her mother's eyes looked just the same, but blank and lifeless, and when her gaze fell on Josie, she did not seem to recognize her either. In one swift movement, her mother bent down so their cheeks were almost touching—their faces so close that Josie could feel the warmth of her breath even as the wind picked up around them. And then she said it, her voice a faint whisper.

"I'm not coming back."

1.

JOSIE TIGHTENED HER PONYTAIL AND WIPED THE SWEAT from her forehead, adjusting her ear band to keep the cold out. The sun was going down and she could now see her breath as she waited at the cross walk. With four miles behind her and one to go, she'd already completed most of her run, but when she'd turned back towards her apartment building, the wind that had been at her back was now pounding her in the face, making it hard to catch her breath.

Three cars went by, their tires sloshing as they moved along the snow-covered street. Finally, the signal changed to show the walking man and Josie made her way across, running again. As dusk settled in, her legs moved faster. She didn't like running in the dark, and in February there wasn't much daylight left once she got home from work in the evening.

As she rounded the last corner into her parking lot, she switched off her music and reached into the key holder on her glove, pulling out the key to her apartment. Her senses intensified when she was alone outside her apartment building—she swore she could hear things no one else could, but tonight everything was quiet. She walked quickly, making her way to Building F, noticing the light post in front of it was flickering in the darkness. This is the stuff horror movies are made of, she thought as she looked over her shoulder again. Were other runners as alert as she became each time she came back from a run? Or, maybe it was just the fact that she was alone, in the dark, with nothing but a key to protect her that had her on edge. Her dad had told her to get some pepper spray to carry with her, or at least to take her cell phone. While she knew she should, she didn't like to carry her phone on her while she ran, and she hadn't gotten around to buying the spray yet.

As she entered the one-bedroom apartment, she quickly shut and locked the door, peering out of the peephole. Her adrenaline was pumping more from her walk across the parking lot than from the actual run, making her feel like she'd run far more than she had. Now safely inside, Josie relaxed. She threw her gloves and ear band onto the black leather sectional that pushed up against the front door's adjoining wall. It had been the first purchase she'd made when she'd moved in. She realized now that its modern design was in direct contrast to the old building, with its many cracks creeping across the ceiling and walls of the place. She'd always tried to see the apartment as charming, but with the dull overhead lighting and fraying carpet, not to mention the tiny bathroom and creaky doors, there were probably other words that better described it.

Pulling her ear buds out, she tossed her jacket onto the couch next, sitting down in the middle of the room to stretch out. Her right calf felt like it was cramping up and she knew she needed to keep it loose. Why hadn't she prepared properly for this run? Not only had she skipped her warmup, but she hadn't had much water to drink before taking off.

Once she felt limber enough, Josie got up and grabbed a water bottle from the fridge—she always kept a few in there ready to go. Refreshed, she walked back over to the couch and sat down, noticing the latest edition of *Catching Up* sitting on the ottoman in front of her. *Catching Up* was Montpier's weekly magazine, filled with restaurant reviews, upcoming events and other newsworthy tidbits that only someone living in or around the area would be interested in. She had picked it up as she left Hayne's Foods with a few sacks of groceries a few days ago, thinking she should get an idea of all the stuff she was missing out on in the city.

Setting her water down on the coffee table, she picked up the weekly pub, its flimsy pages crinkling as she flipped through it. She stopped when she heard a soft buzzing and absently set the magazine down to find her phone.

"Hello?" she answered after tracking it down under a stack of towels in the bathroom. "Dad?"

"Hey, Jo. Just checking in on you."

"Oh," she said, smiling at the sound of his voice. "I just got back from a run." Leaning on the dining table, she untied the laces on her running shoes, grunting as she pulled each one off. The last of the snow she'd failed to stomp off when she entered flew onto the carpet, melting almost immediately.

"In this weather?" His voice wasn't surprised though. He knew how she loved running outdoors, his suggestion to work out on the treadmill falling on deaf ears. Josie didn't run to work out. She ran to clear her mind. Running on a noisy machine sounded about as appealing as watching Monday Night Football. She had no interest in it. Not when she could hop on one of the trails weaving through Montpier and feel her sneakers sloshing on the snow beneath her as she ran.

"It's not so bad when the sun's still out, and I dressed warm enough," she assured him.

"How far today?"

"Around five. I felt pretty good, too, until my leg started giving me some trouble."

He waited for her to continue, but when she didn't he asked, "What kind?"

"Just some cramping. I'm sure I didn't drink enough water today. Busy day at school."

"Aren't they all like that?"

She laughed. He knew her job as a second-grade teacher in Montpier kept her on her toes right up until the bell rang at the end of the day.

"Yeah. I guess they are."

"I was calling to invite you over for dinner this Sunday. Think you'd want to drive on over to Druid Falls to keep your old man company?"

"Sure. What time?"

"Oh, let's say 6:30?"

"See you then."

"Oh, and Josie?"

"Mmm-hmmm?"

"You get that pepper spray yet?"

Darn it. She should've known he'd ask that.

"I'm going to. I just haven't had time."

She could picture him shaking his head before she'd even finished saying it, his mouth puckering into a scowl the way it did when she said something he didn't like.

"You do that. I'd sleep much better at night knowing you have it."

"Alright, Dad. See you Sunday."

"Love you, Jo."

"Love you, too."

She hung up the phone and walked a few paces to the couch to sit down again. It felt good to relax and put her feet up. She remembered the magazine, and picked it up again. It was still open to the last page she had inadvertently flipped to. Scanning the headlines, her eyes fell on a list of volunteer organizations. She read them slowly—Habitat for Humanity, Animal Rescue League—before stopping on one she wasn't familiar with. My Mentor & Me. There was a contact, email address and website listed, along with a short description. *A unique opportunity to offer a one-on-one relationship to a child under the jurisdiction of the Juvenile Court. Become a positive influence in a young person's life today!* Sounded interesting. But she was already struggling to find time in her day, and when she got home at night she usually did schoolwork while watching bad reality shows with the volume turned down.

As she looked through the rest of the magazine, she found herself flipping back and rereading that same text. *Become a positive influence.* Wasn't that what she did every day at her job? Besides, to be a mentor, you had to have life experience. You had to be older. And settled. Josie was just out of college, in a new job and definitely not settled. Still, she found herself contemplating it. Maybe this was just the kind of thing she needed in her life. She went to the kitchen, opening the drawer beside the stove to search out some scissors. She cut the blurb out then hung it on the refrigerator underneath her Eat. Sleep. Run. magnet. She admired it there, the words popping out at her as if they were calling her name. Then she turned and headed to the shower.

"McCray, what are you still doing here?"

Josie looked up from her desk to see Ben Connelly standing in the doorway of her classroom. She motioned to the paper plates, heart cutouts and stickers surrounding her.

"Tell me again why I teach second grade." Josie sighed, raising her eyebrow at Ben, who to Josie's dismay, looked amused. Valentine's Day was tomorrow and she had been stalling. Arts and crafts were not her strong suit.

"Because tomorrow when you see those huge toothy smiles, it will all be worth it."

Ben leaned against the wall, and crossed his arms. He was in his early thirties, with a head full of thick, brown hair, and a penchant for giving Josie a hard time. He was the first person Josie had met when she took the job at Montpier Elementary. She'd walked into the school for her interview just in time to see him spill coffee down the front of his shirt. Almost immediately, they had hit it off, in Josie's opinion, because she gladly accepted anyone clumsier than herself into her inner circle.

"I can't argue with that," she said. "Are you doing anything for yours?"

The Blue Jay

"I had Sway help me," he touted. "She had pinned a bunch of stuff on Pinterest and, lucky for me, she was willing to do some of the labor as well."

Sway Roberts was Ben's unemployed roommate. While not unemployed by choice—she had eventually been replaced at the clinic she worked at after she'd had to cut back her hours to attend to her ailing grandmother—Josie was starting to wonder how she was paying her rent, or if, given his generous nature, Ben was helping her through a rough time.

"I need a Sway," Josie said. "How did you find her again?"

"Facebook, actually. Friend of a friend. You can't go wrong with roommate recommendations from your friends."

Josie laughed. "True. Maybe I should send out a Valentine's Day SOS."

Ben looked down at the few valentines she had finished.

"Oh, you're doing alright." Then he laughed, whipping his phone out to look at the time. "You just might be out of here by midnight."

"You laugh, but it's true. I'll be kicking myself in the morning when I'm running on four hours of sleep."

"You want some help?"

Josie shook her head. While she appreciated the offer, she was not going to make him suffer because of her own procrastination.

"No way. You go. I'll get it done."

"Are you sure?"

"Yes. I'll be fine. Tell Sway I expect her help for St. Patrick's Day, though."

"I'll tell her, but she mentioned going to Chicago with Robbie sometime in the next month so you'll want to let her know if you plan to utilize her services."

"So the blind date was a success?"

"It was. I haven't met him yet, but I think they've seen each other every day since. I just hope the relationship moves slowly enough that I hang onto my very clean, very organized roommate a little while longer."

"Your free teacher's assistant is more like it," Josie chided.

Ben shrugged. "I need all the help I can get. I don't have a Pinterest account. I rely on the ladies in my life to help me out."

"Well, mention it to her at least. Otherwise I'll be spending March 16 in this very same spot," she said.

"I will," he said, giving her a wave as he walked out the door. "See you tomorrow."

"See you," she said, turning back to her project.

By the time Josie gathered up her things to leave, the building was mostly empty. The other teachers on her team—Thresia Morgan and Claire Taylor—had gone long before. Thresia, the oldest of the group with an affinity for books that Josie envied, had worked at Montpier for nearly 20 years. Every year she brought books for teachers to go through for their classrooms—from early readers to chapter books to plays and comic books. It seemed she had an endless supply of them. Claire, a robust woman with a preference for fragrant perfume, had been at the school for 12 years. While one of Josie's close confidants at Montpier, she was also a busy mom with four kids at home. The three of them made an unlikely trio, but in work, they were an enviable team. They gelled together so well, most wouldn't have guessed that Josie was such a new addition to the group.

As she walked to her car, Josie reached into her purse to check her phone. Three missed calls. That's odd, she thought. They were all from Mia. Quickly she punched in Mia's name, wondering if there was an emergency.

"Sweet Josie!" Mia exclaimed when she picked up a few seconds later. It was an expression Mia had used for years, and Josie smiled at the familiarity of it. "Where have you been?"

"Mia, I'm so sorry. Is everything okay? I've been so busy with…"

Mia didn't let her finish. "I'm pregnant!"

"What?" Josie asked, a relieved smile spreading across her face as she realized the news Mia had needed to tell her was of the good variety. She wasn't surprised that her friend just blurted it out like that. She had done the same almost eight years before after her first college class. Josie had called her back, after sneaking her phone into her high school's bathroom to hear all about it. "I'm going to marry the T. A.," Mia had announced—and she'd done just that. She usually did what she said she was going to do. Now, she and James lived in Colorado where he worked as an adjunct professor at a community college and she did PR for an upscale ski resort.

"Hello? Anybody there? I said I'm having a baby!"

It was moments like these when Josie hated that they lived so far apart. She wanted to crawl through the phone and scream and giggle and jump up and down in excitement with her friend. "That's amazing! Congrats to you and James."

"Thank you, Jo. It's early. I'm not quite 12 weeks along," she paused before she continued, "I couldn't not tell you. You're like my sister!"

"I'm so glad you did." Josie responded as she put the key into the ignition of her '04 Ford Focus. With close to 150,000 miles, it had seen its share of driving calamities. For now, it still ran well, and she planned to drive it for as long as she could.

"Now it's your turn," Mia prompted. "What has kept me waiting all day from telling you sooner about my little bun?"

"I know, I'm sorry. I just don't have a minute during the day, and then I had to finish stuff for the party once I got rid of Ben..."

"Got rid of him? Why would you do that?"

Here we go, Josie thought. She never should have mentioned Ben to Mia. Since Josie had started working at Montpier, Mia had been determined to find out why this allegedly handsome man who—bonus—was great with kids had not become a regular fixture in Josie's life.

"Mia, it's not like that. How many times do I have to tell you we're just friends? I work with him. And I don't have time to date right now."

"You always say that. You know you'll never find someone if you don't start making an effort."

"I know it. But Mia, I'm happy with my life right now. I'm settling into a routine, getting used to having my own classroom. I've got a lot going on and a relationship would just complicate everything."

"If you say so."

Mia was not one to like alone time, and really, how could she? She had grown up in a home without any, where every room in the house was occupied by another person. What she did understand was Josie's knack for pushing away anything that might put her in a vulnerable position, anything that could rob her of another piece of her heart.

Josie knew if she was going to change the subject, she'd better do it now before Mia started to grill her more about her lacking love life. "So, when do you find out if this baby's a boy or a girl?"

"May, I think."

"And you'll need to do some shopping for him or her at that point…"

"Um, yeah, probably…"

"So when should I book my trip? I mean, you'll need help carrying all those shopping bags when you go crazy at Carter's, won't you?"

"Sweet Josie! Are you serious?"

"Serious as a heart attack."

"Have I told you lately how much I love you?"

"Only every time I talk to you."

"Well, I do—love you."

"I want to be a part of this, Mia. State lines be damned."

"Then let's do June. By then I'll know for sure, and you'll be out of school. You'll be able to run the trails around here, too, and who knows, I might even go with you."

"Do you mean to tell me that a Shoning is going to do physical activity?"

"Hey now, I took a yoga class last fall. And, you forget, I'm not a Shoning anymore."

Josie kept forgetting that small detail. "One yoga class?"

"It was free. They were running a promotion."

Josie pictured her friend posing on a yoga mat, checking her cell phone every few minutes, or trying to make conversation with the person next to her. Mia was probably not the first person she thought of when picturing the embodiment of serenity.

Some things never change, Josie thought. "Okay, June it is!"

"Let me know what dates end up working and I'll take a few days off of work, too."

"Will do. Congrats again, Mia."

"Thanks, Jo."

Long after they'd ended their conversation, Josie couldn't stop smiling. She pictured Mia holding her newborn baby, and even James learning to change a diaper. They would, undoubtedly, become phenomenal parents. It was only after she'd begun to drift off that she wondered if her own mother had ever felt the same joy she'd heard in Mia's voice tonight. But, she didn't have time to linger on it. Exhausted, her thoughts faded away and she fell into a deep, deep sleep.

2.

The next day was a blur of activity. A shortened schedule to make time for their end-of-day party had her students in such a state, she found herself checking the clock repeatedly. She raised her voice so many times that by the time the party rolled around, she sounded like she was fighting off a bad case of bronchitis.

"Josie." Thresia was standing outside her room, her arms around two of her students. "I found these two throwing candy wrappers at a few of mine."

"Tyler, Abigail, is that true?" They nodded, looking at the floor. "It looks like you'll be staying in from recess next Monday."

"Aww, but Miss McCray, we just wanted to take a valentine to Gwen and Elliott," Tyler said. He was one of Josie's best students, but had a knack for getting into trouble.

"You know the rules. You can't be sneaking in and disrupting Mrs. Morgan's class. And how is throwing candy wrappers giving someone a valentine?" Tyler shrugged. She stole a glance at Abigail who, unlike Tyler, rarely got into trouble. In fact, she looked like she was ready to cry. Josie put a hand on her shoulder in an effort to comfort her—not too much, but enough to hopefully stave off any tears. "Apologize to Mrs. Morgan and then get back to your seats."

"Sorry, Mrs. Morgan," they said in unison, running back to their desks before Josie could delegate any more punishments.

Thresia gave her a knowing wave, then headed back to her own classroom to make sure her students weren't getting out of control, which knowing Thresia, they weren't.

Josie handed out her valentines—she'd made the students party hats out of paper plates. Each one was cut so that when they put it on, a large heart stuck up in front. Josie passed out stickers, markers and colored pencils, and the students began to decorate their hats. Half an hour later, she had them all lined up, in their heart hats, ready to deliver valentines to the other two second-grade classrooms.

In the hallway, they passed Claire's students as the two switched rooms.

"Josie, you continue to outdo yourself," Claire said as they passed each other. "Those hats are precious. I'm going to have to steal that idea for next year, you know."

"Oh, go right ahead! It wasn't hard, just time consuming."

"Well, it's a good one."

Once the party was over and the students had left for the day, Josie wandered down the hall and past the library to the sixth grade classrooms. The building was drafty—the opening and closing of doors from the students leaving put a chill in the air—and she wished she had worn something warmer. The only red item of clothing she owned was a red tank dress, so she had slipped it on with some black tights and a long black sweater for the festivities. Unfortunately, the sweater's material was so lightweight it was almost see-through and had her wishing she had just scrapped the red altogether.

"What are you doing skulking about our wing?" Ben joked when he saw her. He held an old rag in his hand and a spray bottle in the other as he stood at the whiteboard. "They went a little crazy during the party today." There were hundreds of hearts drawn across it, with a few skulls and ninjas thrown in for good measure. Josie guessed that sixth grade boys weren't particularly fond of the Hallmark-inspired holiday.

"I'm not skulking," Josie said, taking a seat at one of the desks in the front row. She leaned back, folding her arms defiantly in front of her.

"So, you're stalking." He paused, turning to look at her, a playful smile on his face. Josie knew he was flirting with her, but she tried to ignore it.

"Not stalking. Just looking for some advice."

"Soliciting, then. I suppose I can help with that. What's up?" He finished cleaning off the board and took a seat at one of the desks beside her.

"Here's the thing," she said, unsure of whether to go on, but also feeling pulled to do so. Ben waited for her to continue. He was looking at her with absolute interest, and she suddenly felt safe, at least safe enough to share this with him. "So I'm thinking of becoming a mentor."

"Really?" His eyes widened just a tad as he said it.

"Yeah," she said. "I think it'd be good for me, and well, good for the kid, too, obviously."

"Obviously."

"I'm serious, Ben. Sometimes I feel like I want to do more for my students, but we don't really get involved in their lives in a more personal way."

"Because we can't."

"Yes, because we have to keep certain boundaries. And I guess, I don't know, I just want to do more. I want to be able to really be there for someone, help them grow into whoever it is they're supposed to become. Not just as my student, but as a person."

"I think that's great, Jo. I really do. What's the problem?"

"I'm just worried. I mean, some days I feel frantic trying to keep up with my work, getting over to Druid Falls to check in on my dad, and making time to fit in a run. I don't know how some teachers do it. I mean, look at Claire. She's got four kids.

The Blue Jay

She's always running from one thing to the next, looking frazzled, but somehow always managing everything. And here I am wondering if I have enough time to devote an hour or two a week."

Ben laughed. "You can't compare yourself to Claire. She thrives on chaos."

"True enough," Josie agreed. He was right. Claire wouldn't know what to do with herself if she had too much free time.

"What you're really worried about is committing to this without thinking it through. You're afraid you might disappoint someone."

"Yes, exactly. I don't want to do it only to find out that I can't devote enough time. I don't want to let someone down when they've probably already been let down plenty."

"Understandable. But you know, if something means enough, you make time." He met her eyes briefly. "And it sounds to me like this means something to you."

She nodded. "It does."

He tilted his head back, putting his hands up around his neck and closed his eyes, thinking.

"Why don't you include him or her in something you're already doing?" he asked.

"What do you mean?"

"Well, take your running. You pretty much go every night, right?"

"Usually."

"It's great exercise. It clears your head. You even sign up for races occasionally?"

"Uh-huh."

"So, there's a sense of accomplishment from competition. It's perfect."

"You think we should run together?"

"Sure. Why not?"

"Wouldn't that be like, child labor or something?"

Ben laughed. "Child labor? Are you kidding? It's running. And it's not like you're going to be running marathons." He straightened up and looked at Josie, suddenly serious. "You're not, are you?"

"No," she said, laughing. "5K queen right here." She was quiet for a moment, considering this. "I was hoping to be paired up with a fifth or sixth grader. They can run a few miles easy, right?"

Ben's face broke out into a smile. "That's the spirit."

"Thanks, Ben," she said, standing up to leave. "You know, I should stop by here more often if you're going to be giving out such decent advice."

"Anytime," he said, before adding, "I hope you will."

She could feel her face flush as she made her way back to her room, and this time she wasn't entirely certain it was because of the cold.

By the time Sunday rolled around, Josie was eager to see her dad. Since her conversation with Ben, she'd been thinking a great deal about what becoming a mentor would mean, and how it would affect her life, and she was beginning to run out of reasons why it wasn't a good idea.

When she pulled up to the house, she stalled a moment, taking in the familiar images of her youth. The house was idyllic, in the sense that it had the look of a typical small-town house. It was a gablefront, with two small rectangular windows side by side under the gable—one to Josie's old room, one to her dad's. Most of the house was done with a thin vinyl siding, but a triangle at the top of the gable, just above the windows, was done in a small fish-scale accent. Cement steps and metal handrails led up to the portico and screened-in front door. Josie had run up and down those steps a million times, usually with some creature hidden in her cupped hands. The house was a slate color, and Josie guessed that over the years it had faded some from sun exposure even though the big oak still stood in front of it. The trunk of the tree was tall enough that, in summer, its

The Blue Jay

leaves cast shadows over the front of the house and blocked out much of the sun's rays.

Her favorite part of the house was an old cast-iron school bell that sat in between the hostas next to the porch steps. Her father had found it one weekend at an antique store about 20 miles from Druid Falls, and brought it home to show Josie. He had excitedly run inside from a downpour and yelled for her to come with him to the truck. It was one of the few memories she still had that included her mother, who had been baking in the kitchen while Josie played with her dolls on the kitchen floor. She could only have been about four or five at the time. They had both nearly jumped out of their skins when he suddenly entered the house, dripping wet, arms flailing and called for them to come outside. Her mother had shaken her head and gone back to slicing apples for the pie she was making, but Josie had jumped up and ran out to the porch.

"Josie girl!" he had said. She could still see him waving to her, standing out in the rain, completely soaked, a ball of energy and excitement. "Come down and see what I've brought you!"

"But it's raining," she'd said. It had been a typical spring storm and come on suddenly, and would probably pass just as quickly. She held back, knowing her mother wouldn't like her getting all wet.

"This?" he'd asked. "This is nothing! C'mon, Jo. You're too young to be so worried about a little rain."

She had hung back as she watched him make his way back to the truck and start to pull the bell out from its bed. When she saw it she had leapt from the porch and run full blast at him, her eyes wide with curiosity. "Daddy, what is it?"

Turning, he left the bell where it was and crouched to talk to her through the heavy rain. "It's a bell, of course."

"What's it for?"

"Why, to look at. And for your mama to ring you home from Mia's for dinner."

Josie had giggled as the rain soaked her hair and ran down her face.

"Shall we try it out?" She remembered he'd had a twinkle in his eye as he picked her up and placed her in the bed of the truck. "Go on."

Using all of her strength, she'd pulled hard on the crank.

Ding. Ding. Ding.

The clapper had hit the bowl so hard that the sound had made her jump and she'd turned around and dove back into her dad's arms, putting both hands over her ears to drown out the noise.

Chuckling, he pulled them down and asked, "What do you think?"

Josie had hugged him then, wrapping her arms around his neck and squeezing as tight as she could. "It's beautiful."

Now whenever she saw it, she remembered that day. Her mother had barely looked at it when she'd come out of the house to watch them set it at the bottom of the steps. She'd taken in Josie's sopping sundress and said, "You'll be catching a cold for sure now," and walked back inside. Actually, now that she thought about it, Josie couldn't remember her mother ringing the bell even once.

But her dad had used it every night that summer to call her home, and when she'd hear it, she'd tell Mia and the other neighborhood kids that the secret service was calling her for an important mission and run off to jump into her father's arms. Always he'd welcomed her like that, as if it was the first time he'd seen her that day and he couldn't believe what a sight she was. He greeted everyone that way, but with Josie, even more so. He was enchanting, his spirit infectious. Perhaps that's why, when her mother had started turning away when he greeted her the same, she hadn't noticed. Rather than brooding, he'd turned right around and scooped her up instead.

"That was delicious, Dad. Really. A truly great meatloaf." She placed her hand on her stomach and sighed heavily.

"Who are you and what have you done with my daughter?"

Josie laughed. "What do you mean?"

"You've never been a fan of meatloaf."

"Yeah, but I always try it. You never know. Someday I might change my mind."

"And was today the long-awaited day?"

Josie shrugged before playfully shoving his shoulder. "Anyway, if you know I don't like it, and you know I'm coming for dinner, wouldn't that mean you should know better than to make it?"

His eyes lit up. "Not if I thought you might change your mind," he rebuffed. The oven made a clicking sound and they realized they'd forgotten to turn it off. Josie hopped up from her seat and pushed the on/off button.

"So I talked to Mia the other night."

"Yeah?" he looked up from his plate. "What's she been up to?"

"Oh, just the usual, aside from the new addition they'll bring back with them next Christmas."

"Well, I'll be! Mia Shoning is having a baby. Is that what you're telling me?"

"It is."

"My, oh my," he said, shaking his head. "That's great news, Jo. I'm surprised I didn't know actually. I ran into Naomi and Liam at the grocery store the other day, and not a peep. It'd be what, their 12th grandchild?"

"Something like that," Josie said. "I can't remember if Poppy has one or two now. Anyway, Mia said she wasn't quite 12 weeks, so maybe they don't even know. I can't imagine Naomi being able to keep that secret, but maybe that's why she hasn't told them yet."

"Well, that's something." He was quiet a moment, thinking. "So, you're planning to go out there to visit soon?" He knew his daughter well.

"Of course," Josie replied. "I've been saving up to go see Mia and James anyway. I'm guessing it might be later in June, before the baby comes. One last hurrah before the world changes, that kind of thing."

"That sounds grand."

Her dad got up from his seat and started to carry dishes over to the sink. Being older, the house didn't have a dishwasher. And now that Josie had moved out he didn't see the need for one, with it just being him using the dishes.

"Let me help with those, Dad."

They stood at the sink—him washing, her drying and putting things away—and talked about all the goings on in Druid Falls. Her father was a regular gossip and had made it his duty to know everyone's business. Part of it was probably loneliness, part of it curiosity. He liked feeling connected to people, and wasn't one to shy away from asking questions, appropriate or not.

"I've been thinking about becoming a mentor," Josie said once they'd finished the dishes and her dad had poured her a steaming cup of apple cider.

Her father was still standing at the counter, pouring himself a cup, but he put down the ceramic pitcher he was holding and turned to look at her. "What does that mean exactly?"

"Well, I'll be paired up with a child in Montpier, probably not one that's a student in my building, but maybe Southwoods or Kramer—they're both on my side of town, and we'll hang out, do things together. I'll try to be a role model to him or her, be there if they have questions about life or problems they're trying to sort out. Basically I'll be a friend, but instead of the friendship happening organically, we're partnered up."

"I see," Her dad smiled, taking a seat beside her and setting his cup down on the table in front of him. "Jo, you never cease to amaze me."

"What do you mean?"

"I mean, the way you've turned out."

Josie took a sip of her cider, then looked up from her cup, ruminating over the comment.

"Did you think I would turn out like her?"

"Never," he said, letting the word slip easily off his tongue without hesitation. Josie waited for him to go on. "It's hard to explain," he said, finally. "But your mother always had a piece of herself that she kept hidden away. When I first met her, she was a firecracker, but she would also get quite morose at times, and I would have a hard time trying to snap her out of it. It was like she went away in her mind for a bit. She always came back, but as time went on, it took longer for her to find the cheery part of herself again."

He paused, searching Josie's face to see if he should continue. Josie noticed the lines in his own face seemed more creased on this visit, and it hit her that her father, the man with boundless energy, was getting older. It suddenly made their conversation seem more urgent, that there was still so much between them that had never been said.

"When you were born, that sunny part of her came back tenfold. I loved her for it, but I loved you even more for bringing that joy to her—to us, really. Those early years were some of the best in my life. But, as time passed, she started to drift off more and more. You were always so sweet about it. I don't think you even noticed half the time. You'd be playing in your room or running around with Mia. But there were nights I'd come home from work and find her sitting at the kitchen table, just staring out the window. I'd try to talk to her, and she'd look at me like she didn't know who I was. Eventually, I realized that things were probably worse than ever. It took a long time before I realized that I couldn't force her into happiness, and when I finally did it was hard to accept. But while I couldn't fix things for her, I could protect you from seeing it. I decided right then that I would do whatever I could to shield you from it. We never fought, you know. Your mother and I."

Josie nodded. "I know, Dad. That's why when she left, I couldn't understand."

"I tried my damnedest to make sure you didn't notice the bad stuff, that you had a mother just like any other. Whenever she fell into one of those states, I'd bundle you up and take you sledding, or you remember all those evening walks in the summers?"

"Some of my favorite memories."

"Mine too. I just wish she could have been part of them. We'd come home and you'd tell her where we'd been and what you'd seen. Then you'd hug her and skip off, happy as a clam. You never saw the indifference in her. Your naiveté shielded you from it, which was a blessing."

"But then she left."

He sighed, folding his hands in his lap, his head bowing as if in prayer. "I never faulted your mother. She was just the way she was, and I don't think she could have helped it. But, that morning when you ran into my room," he paused. "I've never wanted to hurt another person so much in my life. That she did that to you. That you had no idea why, and I couldn't explain it to you. Hell, it was partly my fault that you didn't see it coming."

Josie reached out for her father's hands. He looked the oldest she had ever seen him, tired even.

"But, Dad, you were perfect that day." He looked up, curious. Josie nodded. "Yeah, you were. I'll admit it was one of the worst mornings of my life. I hate to even think about it, but when I do, you know what I remember? I remember you looking around, realizing what had happened. You brushing the tears off my face and bringing me downstairs, plopping me on the kitchen counter and opening cupboards, taking out all the ingredients for my favorite chocolate chip pancakes. You just started handing me things off of shelves, and then you put on that Sinatra song, "That's Life"—you remember it? You started singing and dancing as you poured everything together. By the time you put the chocolate chips into the batter, I had stopped crying and started dancing and twirling around you."

"I'd forgotten that."

"When the pancakes were finished, you set me on your lap and you said 'Josie girl, this is where we wipe our tears away and we carry on, because we've got to. No one else is gonna do it for us. We'll be just fine, you and I.' and I trusted you to my core, Dad. I knew we would be. That's what I try to remember about that day. Not that I lost a parent, but that I had an amazing one to pick me up."

"We surely did just that, didn't we?" His eyes were twinkling. He leaned back in his chair, looking pleased. "All I know is some lucky boy or girl is going to get one hell of a mentor."

"So you think I should do it?"

"You bet I do."

Josie got up to rinse the last remaining cider from her cup. She turned back around as she put some soap into it to see her dad looking out the window, and she could hear him singing softly. She could just make it out over the running water as she dried off her cup.

"'Cause this fine old world, it keeps spinnin' around."

3.

When Josie returned home that night, she immediately emailed the contact at My Mentor & Me. Surprisingly, she received a message back right away, asking her to submit an application, which she did. They requested three letters of recommendation, so she asked Mia, Ben and her principal to write and send letters in on her behalf. A few weeks later she found herself driving to her one-on-one meeting with the match coordinator.

As she walked into the small office, Josie was pleased to see that they had been expecting her. A man and a woman looked up as she entered, gesturing for her to come in, and her nerves quickly subsided. She approached them eagerly and shook their hands.

"You must be Josie McCray," the woman said, smiling. "I'm Katherine, the match coordinator here at My Mentor and Me." She was young, just a few years older than Josie, and she was holding a file with Josie's name on it. "This is Oliver," she said, gesturing to the man to her left. "Our executive director."

"It's nice to meet you both," Josie said.

"We're really glad to have you," Oliver said. "I won't keep you, but I do like to meet all of our potential mentors myself—to ease any fears they may have and just make sure they know how needed they are."

"Of course," Josie said, then adding, "I'm really excited about this."

"You're a teacher, right?"

"I am."

"Well, this will be a breeze for you then."

"I don't know about that," Josie laughed, shoving her hands deep into her pockets. "At school I've got 25 little ones running around needing attention, so it'll be a bit of a change to put so much focus into just one."

"What grade do you teach?" he asked. He seemed genuinely interested and it made Josie feel incredibly welcome.

"Second."

"I bet that's a handful. Most of the kids in our program are older, although we do have some younger ones. I believe Katherine has three profiles to go over with you that could be potential matches."

"That's right," Katherine agreed. "Hopefully we'll be able to make a match today."

"Josie," Oliver started as he pushed his glasses up on his nose and reached to shake Josie's hand again. "It was very nice to meet you. I'll let you get to it."

With that, he grabbed his coat and was out the door. Katherine led Josie into her office, a small cozy space that was made homier by the small desk lamp next to her computer. Sitting down at her desk, she flipped open Josie's file, her perfectly manicured fingers flying through the first few pages in the folder.

"Things get moving a bit quicker now that we've received your application and all three letters of recommendation. We've already run your background check—that obviously checked out fine. Now all that's left to do is choose the child you want to work with. As Oliver said, I've pulled three files to go over with you today. They include backgrounds of each child, things like their name, any issues they may be currently dealing with, parent involvement, if any, and a simplified overview of what the child has been going through in the past few months."

MICHELLE SCHLICHER

Katherine stopped and circled some things on the paper in front of her, then turned it so that Josie could see.

"Our volunteers are asked to spend a minimum of six hours a month with their mentee. Weekly contact by phone, email or in person are all options, although in person is best. Anything that adds a regular routine to their life is beneficial—if you can see the child more, then that's great. But we also understand that people are busy. We don't want you to overpromise and then have to cancel plans, so we tell our mentors to really think about how much time they can devote and when."

"A lot of these children are missing out on things that don't seem exciting to you and me. They're probably things you wouldn't think to include them in, but are just the types of things that will benefit them in the long run—grocery shopping, yard work, washing your car. Just normal, everyday things."

"That makes sense," Josie said.

"Do you have any questions so far?"

Josie thought for a moment. She was excited to begin this process, but she also knew the children and teens in this program needed people who would be in their lives for the long haul. "How long does a typical match relationship go on?"

Katherine smiled, folding her hands in front of her on the desk.

"That all depends on the mentor and his or her mentee. We ask our volunteers to commit to at least six months, but many of them go on much longer. The best-case scenario would be that your match becomes a part of your life and the relationship evolves the same way that any other relationship you have does. There are matches that don't work out, and in those instances we can re-place you. Our main concern is to make the best possible match for the child and the mentor. We don't want either party stuck in something that's not working."

"Sure," Josie said, her heart racing in her chest. "I don't want that either."

"Okay," Katherine flipped through a few more of the pages in front of her, then looked up at Josie, grinning. "This is my favorite part. Let's match you up!"

Josie nodded, biting down on her lip anxiously.

"Up first—Payton Runnells, male, 12 years old. He's been in foster care for about a year. Actually, he's being placed with a new family in the next week or so. He's had a lot of changes in the past few months. No parent involvement since his mom left. His teachers have told his caseworker that he's been struggling a bit in school with grades and there's been some fighting. Nothing physical, but worrisome nonetheless."

"Is there a father in the picture?"

Katherine shook her head. "No, it was just him and his mom. He entered foster care when she failed to pick him up at school one day."

"Next up is..."

"Wait," Josie muttered.

Katherine looked up. "Did you say something?"

"That's okay." She said it louder. "I'll take him."

"You don't want to hear the others?"

"I don't think I need to." She paused, contemplating what she'd just said. "You said he was fighting a bit, but that you weren't worried. He's not dangerous or anything, is he?"

"No, we wouldn't match you up if he was likely to become physical with you." Katherine lifted an eyebrow. "Are you sure you don't want to hear the other profiles?"

"Yes. I think he'll be fine. I think I might be able to relate to him well." She paused before continuing, feeling the heat rise to her cheeks. She didn't know why it was so hard to admit, but it still was after all this time. "My mom left when I was young, too."

"Ah, I see." She didn't look at Josie in pity or give her the sad, droopy eyes. In fact, Katherine didn't seem fazed at all and moved right along. Josie liked her all the more for it. "Well, that may have been the fastest match I've ever done. I'll work with

Payton's new foster family and coordinate a time for all of us to meet. It may take a bit longer because of him switching residences, but I'll see what I can do."

"So that's it?"

"That's it," Katherine said. As Josie stood up to leave, Katherine suddenly stopped her. "Josie, this is a great thing you're doing. We have an unfortunately long waiting list with more and more kids being added to it all the time. Mentoring can be a thankless job, especially at first, so I'm saying it right now. Thank you."

Embarrassed, Josie fidgeted uncomfortably and mumbled, "You're welcome."

Katharine walked her to the door, holding it open as Josie stepped through. "I'll be in touch soon."

The rest of the week flew by. There were lesson plans to develop, assignments to grade, and a professional development literacy workshop to attend, so when Ben suggested she meet him for drinks that Friday with Sway, she welcomed the break from anything to do with school. They had planned to meet at Flannigan's at five, but Josie didn't pull into the parking lot until almost half past.

"Josie, you made it!" Sway gave her a tight hug as she slid into the booth next to her.

"We thought you were standing us up," Ben added, winking at Sway.

"I'm sorry you guys," Josie said. "I got a call from an angry parent, and I guess he just needed to blow off some steam or something. I could not get him off the phone. His son is having some trouble with, well, lots of things, and he wasn't happy about my referral. I hated to brush him off right before the weekend, so I just let him keep talking. I mean, I could understand why he'd be upse…"

"Josie," Sway interrupted, holding up a finger a few inches from Josie's face. "You are officially too nice. Not only that, but it's finally the weekend. Now is the time to de-stress."

"In other words, not talk about work," Ben said.

"Right," Josie said, trying to clear her mind. She took a deep breath and relaxed her shoulders. "So, what did I miss?"

"You missed Ben moping about his sweet ride."

"What's wrong with your ride?" Josie asked, turning her attention to Ben and making herself comfortable. He was leaning back in the booth taking a sip of his beer.

"Ol' Bess just doesn't have much left in her. I'm going to have to trade her in soon."

"Finally," Sway said. "Every time I see that car, I think to myself, why isn't that mother out picking her kids up from soccer practice? Then I remember it's yours."

"Hey now, I bet there's quite a few good-looking guys out there driving a Vibe."

"Yeah, the girls go gaga over a guy in a station wagon."

"It's not a station wagon," Ben protested. Then turning to Josie, he added, "It doesn't matter anyway. I'm going to have to get something new."

Josie had ridden in the red and gray Pontiac a few times before when her own beater had failed her, and Ben had given her a ride to school. It had seemed like a fine car to her, but then she drove an old car, too, albeit, not a station wagon. "I'm sure you'll find something fantastic," Josie said, before adding, "Not mom-tastic, fantastic. Just want to be clear." Sway giggled beside her.

"Very funny, you two," Ben said. "Well, I won't be consulting either of you on my next purchase."

"No, I think that means you should be consulting us," Sway said. "So you don't make the same mistake twice."

"Or worse, and end up with a beetle convertible," Josie added.

Sway gasped, "The ultimate girl car!"

Josie laughed, the tension finally leaving her body. She was glad they had chosen Flannigan's. While they couldn't enjoy the rooftop patio during the winter, the atmosphere was laid-back and they had one of the best tenderloins in town, so big that it was twice the size of the bun it was served on.

"So, Sway," Josie said, changing the subject. "Are you and Robbie going to be taking that romantic excursion Ben was telling me about soon?"

"You mean Chicago?" Sway started playing with the label on her Guinness, and Josie thought it might have been the first time she'd ever seen Sway blush in embarrassment. "I wouldn't call it a romantic excursion, but yes, we are. Downtown Chicago for St. Pat's. I've never been, so yeah, I think it will be fun. He's got friends there and we're going to stay with them." She was trying to downplay her excitement, but her eyes lit up as she talked about it. "I'm honestly surprised. I mean, he's not at all how my friend Ashley described him to me before she set us up."

"He's way cooler," Ben said. He playfully rolled his eyes and took a swig of his Newcastle.

"Benjamin Connelly! That is just rude." Sway threw her paper napkin at him.

"Hey, I'm glad you guys hit it off. But, I'm not gonna lie. I'll be sad if it's true love and you leave me to shack up with him instead."

"I think you'd survive." Sway said. "On second thought I did find a week-old takeout box of Thai food in the fridge today. I'm sure if I wasn't there to throw it out, it would've still been there a month from now."

"Oh, I'm not that bad," Ben refuted. "Am I?"

"You might be," Josie said. "There's always Thai takeout in the teacher's lounge, and none of us are ever sure how old it is."

"Dang. This is just not my night."

"Okay, we'll lay off," Sway said, patting his hand from across the table. "Anyway, Josie, to answer your question, yes, we're taking a trip and I'm very excited about it. There's an aide that's going to be checking in on my Grams, too, so that's all set."

"How is your grandma?"

"She's spry as ever. I try to tell her she needs to take it easy, but she's always moseying around the assisted living residence getting all the latest gossip on everyone. She's only been there six months, but she knows everything."

"My dad would be the same," Josie said, though she couldn't imagine him old enough to be in one.

A waitress finally came by the table and took Josie's drink order. After several minutes of deliberation, she decided to order the tenderloin as well. Ben and Sway followed suit, with Sway ordering an extra to take to Robbie later. By the time they finished eating, Josie's week was behind her and she was feeling pretty mellow.

"So, Josie, Ben mentioned some kind of mentoring thing. Have you started that yet?"

"Next week. There was some holdup with his caseworker because he's moving to a new foster home. But yeah, it's coming up."

"Do you know anything about him?" she asked.

"Not much. Just that his mom left. He's been in some trouble, although I'm not sure the extent of it."

"Hmmm," Sway said. "And his dad?"

"Not in his life. I don't think he ever has been."

"Too bad," Ben said. "He goes to Southwoods?"

"I'm not sure, actually."

"Well, if anyone can be a good influence, it's you," Sway said, putting her arm around Josie and squeezing her shoulder.

Josie smiled, but she'd heard it several times now. And the thing was, she wasn't sure she could do it at all. She hoped she'd have an influence, and that it'd be a good one, but she wasn't getting her hopes up either. This boy could hate the world. He could see her as someone that was just like the rest of the people floating in and out of his life. She could fail miserably at this whole endeavor and end up wishing she'd never laid eyes on that blurb in *Catching Up*. Though she wanted to hope for the best, she also felt a bit nervous, and all the faith people had in her made her uneasy. The pressure was beginning to weigh on her and she hadn't even met the boy yet.

"Well, kids, it's been fun, but I've got to get this sandwich to Robbie before his texts start to turn nasty. The boy is a handful when he's hungry." Josie slid off the bench, letting Sway out. "It was really great catching up, Josie. Come by sometime and we'll make Ben watch chick flicks and sing along to Katy Perry. He won't mind, I mean he does drive a *Vibe*."

Ben ignored her, but Josie laughed, hugging Sway and thinking how nice it was to have a girl friend who just accepted her with open arms. Her circle was small, and when Mia had left for Colorado it had left Josie, at times, feeling lonely. "Bye Sway," she said, before sitting back down across from Ben.

"So," Ben said after Sway had gone. "Are you nervous?"

Josie took a sip from her glass. "I am. I didn't think I would be as nervous as I am, but I just have no idea what to expect."

"But it has to be a bit exciting, too."

"It is," she looked around the bar, full of people having a good time, their busy weeks behind them, and the next week still too far off to worry about. "When I think about it, I'm nervous about everything that has to do with him. What will he be like? Will he hate me? Things that I have no control over." Josie rested her eyes on Ben, who was attentive and, she could tell, feeling the effects of the drinks he'd had. "The excitement I feel probably has more to do with me, that I'm finally putting myself out there. And, surprisingly, I'm not scared about that. It's the first time that I've felt like I'll be able to give of myself, and no matter what happens, even if Payton despises me at first, I can still show him that somebody cares."

"He won't despise you, Jo. He'll be on guard, but he'll probably be more curious then anything. Do you want me to call one of my buddies over at Southwoods and do a little digging? Find out a little more about him?"

"No, that's alright. I'm meeting him soon. It's just the anticipation of it that's getting to me. I just want to get started." Josie twirled one of her curls around her finger, searching for a

The Blue Jay

way to tell Ben why she really was so eager to meet Payton. "You know, his mom left. He's been in foster care ever since."

Ben was quiet. He was playing with the label on his bottle, tearing off pieces of it and rolling them between his fingers, making little paper balls. "I see. And you're hoping you'll be able to help him through it?"

"I'm uniquely qualified, don't you think?"

"I do. I just..."

Ben put his bottle down and looked at Josie.

"You just..." Josie prodded.

"I just want you to be careful. You know, his circumstances could be very different from yours. He may not want help at all, ever, and I just hope you won't see it as a failure if that's the case."

"I won't."

"Are you sure?"

Surprised, Josie looked at him. His brow was furrowed, making him look more serious than usual, and his eyes were troubled. She wasn't sure what he was thinking.

"Ben, I've thought a lot about this, going over different scenarios. I know that it might not work out, and if it doesn't, it doesn't. But, I'm also not going to just give up on him right away either. And if I get my ego bruised a bit here and there, I can handle it. Do you think I'm not capable?"

"I think that maybe you have a tendency to keep people at arm's length. And, while it keeps you feeling safe, it also makes you unavailable. Kids are very perceptive. If he gets that from you, he might think it's not worth it. That you'll never totally be yourself with him anyway, so why should he?"

It didn't get past Josie that he used the word unavailable. And while she knew he was right, for some reason she didn't worry about that being a problem with Payton. But, she didn't know how to explain that to Ben. And she wasn't entirely sure he was exclusively talking about Payton, either.

"It's different with this, Ben. I have nothing to lose, here."

"Maybe. At first, anyway. What happens later, when you've grown attached and it doesn't work out?"

Josie didn't know how to answer. She'd been so preoccupied with the prospect of meeting Payton, she hadn't really thought about down the road. Without having met him yet, it was hard to even imagine what things would look like a few months from now.

"You're a bit of a negative Nelly tonight, aren't you?" she said, changing the subject.

"I'm sorry," he said. "I'm not trying to be a downer."

A few minutes later Josie waved down their waitress to get the bill. "I think I'm going to get going," she said to Ben, taking out her wallet and laying it on the table.

"Yeah, I guess I should probably get home, too. Listen, Josie, I'm sorry. I'm just concerned. That's all. I hope that everything goes great with Payton. I'm sure it will. I can't help it that I'm worried, though. I'd be a fool not to worry about you."

Josie chose to ignore the feeling she was hearing in his voice. "Well, I'm a big girl. I'll be fine. I'm prepared for wherever this experience takes me." She could feel her cheeks turning red. Was it from the alcohol—or something else?

"Okay," Ben said. "Well, I'm here if you need me."

They paid their bills and made their way outside. "Thanks for inviting me tonight, Ben. It was just what I needed after a long week."

"Yeah, it was fun. I'll see you Monday, Josie."

"See you Monday."

As she walked across the parking lot she turned back once to see Ben still watching her. She gave him a little wave before getting into her car, thinking about the conversation they'd just had, and the sincere banter between two friends that had suddenly taken on a different tone. What had felt completely innocent before now felt more intimate somehow. Josie's heart was racing and her imminent meeting with Payton was no longer the sole reason.

4.

The blue jay is an aggressive bird, known for tormenting and even attacking other birds and chasing them from feeders—its striking blue coloring a distraction from the fact that it's actually not a nice bird at all. But the blue jay does have one redeeming quality, one that should not be overlooked when considering its temperament. As predatory birds swoop in, a blue jay will scream out, alerting smaller birds and scaring the hawk or owl away, embracing its role as the unlikely protector.

THE DAY JOSIE MET PAYTON RUNNELLS WAS ALSO THE SECOND day he had spent in his third foster home. He had been dropped off after school on Friday. And on Saturday morning, Josie was already pulling into an established neighborhood of historic homes and tree-lined streets to meet him. To say he was apathetic to meeting her would be an understatement. But then, Josie hadn't expected their relationship to be easy.

The first thing she noticed upon walking up the sidewalk to the prominent two-story home—she guessed it was built sometime in the 19th century—was the stillness of it. The wind didn't howl. No cars passed by—it was as if this moment, as she slowly made her way up the driveway, trying to gain control of her nerves, was the only one to exist in the world, and her mind was capturing it for her.

She took a deep breath and walked up the stairs to a recently added wrap-around porch and rang the doorbell. A middle-aged man with black-rimmed glasses and a welcoming smile greeted her. He held open the door and waved her in.

"Josie McCray?"

"That's me," Josie replied. "I think I may be a bit early. Katherine said ten o'clock, but I didn't see another car out front."

"Yes, that's alright. Katherine just called. She had some sort of emergency at the office to deal with and is on her way here now. I'm Bernard Grier."

They shook hands as Josie took in the impressive interior of the large house, which looked like it was going through some renovations. While the foyer had updated hardwood flooring and newly-painted taupe walls, a room off to the right of the entryway was outfitted in blue and pink floral wallpaper that looked like it was straight out of the 1930s, perhaps when it was last remodeled by a previous owner. It was a beautiful house, and Josie found herself staring in awe at the intricate design of the Victorian chandelier hanging over them in the entryway, just in front of the staircase leading upstairs.

As she was admiring her surroundings, a woman walked into the foyer.

"Josie, I'm Mae Grier," she said, as she looped her arm into her husband's. She was a smallish woman who wore her brown hair pulled back in a tight bun, making her look older than her husband, as well as a bit more intimidating. "We're so glad to have you. As you know, Payton just arrived here yesterday."

"Yes, I was aware that there had been some trouble at his previous placement, although I don't know the details of that."

Mr. Grier nodded. "He's been fine so far with us, but yes, I think he's had a rough time." He looked at his wife and they exchanged a sympathetic glance. Josie wasn't sure how she felt about it. She had seen a similar look on people not long after her mother had left and she hadn't necessarily liked it then either. "Can I take your coat?"

The Blue Jay

"Oh yes." She slid her arms out and handed it to Mr. Grier.

"Why don't we sit in here?" Mrs. Grier said, motioning for her to follow into room with the unfortunate wallpaper. "We're slowly updating things around here. As you can see we haven't gotten around to this room yet."

"The house is amazing," she said.

"It's been an undertaking," Mr. Grier replied as he joined them. "But this room has kind of grown on me, Mae."

Mrs. Grier laughed. "Knowing how much work will have to go into it, I might just have to agree with you." She turned to Josie. "Please, have a seat. Can I get you anything while we wait for Katherine? Water? Coffee? "

"A coffee would be great."

Mrs. Grier vanished, returning a few minutes later to set an aqua cup and matching saucer down on the end table. "Do you take cream or sugar?"

"Both." Josie said, taking in the aroma that always managed to arouse her senses. Mrs. Grier disappeared into the kitchen again. When she returned, she placed a small cream pitcher and a few packets of sugar on the table in front of Josie. "Thank you."

"You know the best coffee I've ever had was at a cafe in London," Mrs. Grier said after she had handed another cup to her husband. "My sister and I took a trip there last fall. I don't remember the name now, but the staff was so knowledgeable about the process of making it. Anyway, they offered a drink there—a syphon, I think it was called—anyway, it was quite a spectacle to watch them make it."

Josie shifted in her chair as she took a sip from the teal mug. "London, hmm? That is something." She took another sip, savoring the flavor on her tongue, feeling out of her element. The Griers were well-traveled. They lived in a beautiful, historic home. Josie was so far removed from their lifestyle she wasn't quite sure what to say next. "For me, the experience is almost better than the coffee itself—the warm cup, the delicious smells. I don't drink it too often, sometimes after a morning run, but otherwise I try to stay away from too much caffeine. When I do have a cup, it's definitely a treat."

"So, you're a runner?" Mr. Grier sat forward with his elbows resting on his knees. "I used to run back in the day. Hurdles if you can believe it."

Josie could. Mr. Grier was a fit man and definitely looked like he could have been a track star in his earlier years. He was decidedly upbeat, and spoke with an enthusiasm that was more than a little contagious to Josie's delight.

"I run 5K's here and there," answered Josie. "Nothing too ambitious. You'll never see me out doing a marathon, although I did run a half a few years ago."

"It's a great stress reliever. I remember practicing with the team always got my head right after a rough day."

"It is. I teach at the elementary level so my days can get stressful for sure."

"You hear that, Mae?" He looked at Mrs. Grier, who nodded in delight. "Our daughter's a teacher out east. What grade?"

"Second."

"Martha's a kindergarten teacher. I don't know how you do it with all those young kids. It must be quite a handful."

Josie laughed, "Well, I can't speak for your daughter, but I've found that once I fall into a routine and get to know the students, things run pretty smoothly. It helps that they are still scared of visiting the principal's office at that age. And, there's really nothing like it. Even on the hard days, it's invigorating. I'm always surprised by something."

"That's a nice way of looking at it, dear," Mrs. Grier said.

Before Josie could respond, there was a knock on the door. Mr. Grier went to answer it. Katherine, looking frazzled, entered the house and immediately began to apologize for her tardiness. Mr. Grier took her coat, waving her in the direction of the others.

"Josie, Mrs. Grier," she said, upon entering. "I am so very sorry for making you wait."

"It's no problem at all, Katherine. We've just been getting to know Josie here." She nodded in Josie's direction. "And, honestly, we're just glad that things can begin to move forward for Payton's sake as he settles in with us."

"Yes, well, I have every intention of making this as quick and as easy as possible on my end so that Josie and Payton can begin to get to know each other. Payton's here, correct?"

Mr. Grier reentered the room and leaned against the mantel of the fireplace, standing near Katherine, who didn't look like she intended on sitting down quite yet. "Yes, he's in his room reading," he said. "We told him we'd be up to get him when everyone was here."

"Fabulous," Katherine said, still a bit out of breath from her speedy entrance into the house. "Once he's down here, I want to explain a few things to him so that he understands a little more about the program. Then, Josie, we'll set up your first activity together so you both know the next time you'll see each other."

"That works for me," Josie said. Her heart was beating so fast, she felt as if she'd just run the most difficult race of her life.

"I'll go and get Payton," Mrs. Grier said, getting up from the couch and heading to the stairs in the foyer.

Katherine turned her attention to Josie and pulled a folder out of the leather portfolio she had carried in with her.

"I've printed out some contact information for you, including for both Mr. and Mrs. Grier. There are numbers in here for many of the county's crisis and emergency hotlines, as well as some common questions about being a volunteer with us. There's also a list of local activities for you to do together—many mentors wonder what kinds of things they should be doing during their one-on-one time. It's important to know that a trip to the library, going fishing, flying a kite at the park, all of these free activities are just as beneficial as anything that costs money. As I mentioned in our previous meeting we also have group events once a month."

She handed Josie the folder.

"More than anything," she added, "be patient and listen. What he needs most is a friend who has his best interest at heart."

As she finished speaking, Mrs. Grier entered the room, followed by Payton, who seemed to linger in the doorway as he looked around the room. He was wearing a red hoodie sweatshirt that he had pulled up around his head, his fingers twisting the ends of the hoodie's laces. Josie smiled, trying to meet his eyes, but he didn't look up at her.

"Payton, do you remember me? My name is Katherine. I work with My Mentor and Me."

Payton didn't respond, but he looked up at Katherine and stole a quick glance at Josie.

"This is Josie McCray," she said, pointing in Josie's direction. "She's going to be spending some time with you over the next few months."

"Hi, Payton," Josie said, giving him a sincere smile. "I'm so glad to meet you."

Payton looked at her, then scoffed.

"Payton, why don't you come sit over here?" Mrs. Grier motioned for him to join her on the couch, obviously disappointed by his attitude. Payton let go of the strings he was holding and pulled his red hoodie down, revealing a head of hair to complement his shirt—its fiery color standing out against his pale skin.

Once Payton had taken a seat next to his latest foster mom, he looked across at Josie, but didn't say anything. Katherine took the opportunity to pull out a paper and hand it to him.

"This is Josie's contact information. Mr. and Mrs. Grier also have a copy if you happen to misplace this one." Payton nodded, but acted disinterested. Katherine continued. "With My Mentor and Me, we want you to have the opportunity to see each other as little or often as you feel comfortable with so we leave it up to the two of you to decide when and where you'll get together. However, we send out monthly emails detailing

THE BLUE JAY

our group events and any other events around town that may be of interest to you."

Katherine turned to Josie.

"Once you get to know each other a bit more—and especially if you have any shared interests—it will be easier to plan your time together. Payton has told his counselors of his love of reading, so the local library's author series might be one idea."

Josie smiled at Payton and said, "I love to read, too. It's part of why I love being a teacher. Are you reading anything now?"

Payton shrugged, but kept his eyes on Josie. She took this as a good sign, that he wasn't ready to write her off just yet. His curiosity was giving her a small in, so she kept talking.

"I just finished reading *The Giver*. A friend of mine who teaches sixth grade gave it to me."

"A very good book," Katherine added.

"Yes, it is," Josie agreed. "I'm sure he would let you borrow it if you wanted."

Payton returned to fidgeting with the strings on his hoodie. Mr. and Mrs. Grier exchanged their empathetic glances again, frustrating Josie. She wasn't taking it personally. The boy had just moved in with two people he didn't know, and now was being forced to begin another relationship that, to him, was likely temporary.

Katherine was unfazed by his demeanor. She had most likely seen much worse. Josie appreciated her directness, and her consistently upbeat responses.

"How about we set up your first activity? What evenings work best?" She was looking at Payton, but he clearly wasn't going to answer her.

"He's got meetings with his counselor after school on Tuesdays, but any other night should work," Mrs. Grier said, looking at Payton, trying to will him into speaking.

"Josie, when would work for you? What about next week?" Katherine asked.

Josie nodded, taking a small notebook out of her purse and a purple pen she'd accidentally taken from her bank's drive-up window so she could write down these details. "How about Wednesday?" She turned her head from Katherine and looked right at Payton, who was trying his best not to care about the conversation going on around him. "We'll just keep it simple and go for pizza. How does that sound?"

He shrugged.

He didn't look at her when he said it, but at least he'd acknowledged her. It was enough for Josie. There was hope for them both yet.

Later that night, as she drove home from the Griers', Josie thought about the boy she had just met. After her mother had left, Josie had shut down. The only people she had opened up to at all about how she was feeling during that time were her dad and Mia, but those relationships had suffered too, for a while at least. Trust didn't come easy for her then, and she still had to work at it now.

Payton reminded her so much of herself that it scared her. She could see his anger. Hell, she could feel it. It was an anger that was directionless. He was angry at the world, and Josie guessed, he was still holding out hope that his mom would return. When Katherine had told her the circumstances surrounding him being in foster care, she knew it had to be him. If she could relate to any of the kids in the My Mentor & Me program, he would be the one. But there was a part of her that was afraid of him, too. Because while she'd still had her dad when her mom left, Payton had no one, making him much more vulnerable than even she could understand.

5.

"How did it go?" Claire asked when she arrived at school the next week.

Josie pulled the black-and-white scarf from around her neck as she unbuttoned her coat. Claire must have seen her walk in, and hurried over to catch her before their students started to arrive. That was one thing about Claire. She always remembered the big things. The little things, like where she put her keys or what time her students had art class, which she was notoriously late for, would consistently be forgotten. But the big things? She was more than on top of those.

"Was he happy to meet you?"

"I wouldn't say he was happy, but it wasn't terrible. He didn't say anything at all, actually, so I really can't even tell you much about him. His foster parents are nice, but I don't know how close they'll be able to get."

"That's too bad."

Josie shrugged and grabbed a pen off her desk, jotting down a reminder to pick up her dry cleaning. "We're going for pizza this Wednesday."

"Pizza sounds divine," Claire said, patting her stomach. "Phil took Eric and Ava to daycare this morning. I hurried them all out the door with a banana in hand. Then, Kellie and Lauren needed to get to the bus stop, so I threw a package of Pop Tarts to them as they got their boots on. I didn't have time to get myself something. Thank goodness I keep some granola bars in my desk. I tell you, Josie, sometimes I wonder how I make it here on time."

"Sometimes I wonder how you make it here on time," Josie said. "I'd be running around like a crazy person and show up here with mismatched socks or my shirt inside out."

"Don't think I haven't done both of those things."

Josie laughed. "Well, you hide it well."

"Between you and me, I don't know how Phil talked me in to trying for our boy. I should have known we'd end up with twins." She was shaking her head in disbelief, but you could see the contentment on her face. She loved those kids more than anything. "Thankfully, Eric is the sweetest boy I've ever laid eyes on, and his sister is, unlike her older sisters, the easiest baby, so I shouldn't complain. I'm not complaining, really. Just some mornings feel like a race to the finish, only I'm going in the wrong direction. Ya know what I mean?"

"I'm pretty sure most people feel like that about Monday mornings," Josie assured her.

"I suppose. Well, I better get back to my room."

After Claire had left, Josie began to pass out spelling worksheets, laying them on the small desks spread throughout the classroom. As her students entered the room and made their way to their seats, she felt a wave of energy that sustained her for the rest of the day. She only hoped it would sustain her through Wednesday, too.

"So, how has it been going at the Griers'?"

Josie wasn't sure he would answer. He'd barely said two words since she'd picked him up and they'd driven across town to Vito's Place. Now they were seated in a giant red booth in the small, family-owned pizza house, and Josie had just ordered them a deep dish pepperoni pizza.

He didn't answer, instead looking down at the table.

"And school? Are you studying anything interesting in your classes?"

He shrugged, refusing to meet her eyes.

Well, this wasn't going anywhere, she thought. She looked at the table next to them. There were two little girls laughing, standing on their chairs and being shushed by their parents. The mother was mid-bite when she realized one of the girls had picked food up off the floor. She barely had time to swat it out of the girl's hand before she devoured it. Across the restaurant sat an elderly couple, waiting for their pizza, talking in hushed voices. Another couple, teenagers, looked to be on a date. They all looked so relaxed. Not anything like what Josie imagined she and Payton looked like—her a nervous wreck and him quietly staring at his hands in his lap.

"Do you want to know anything about me?" Josie asked.

He didn't respond.

"I'll just tell you a little bit about myself. I'm not sure how much Katherine told you."

She took a sip from her pop, then pushed the straw up and down between the ice cubes.

"I'm a second-grade teacher at Montpier Elementary. I'm originally from Druid Falls. Have you heard of it?" No answer. "I like to run, mostly 5K's, but sometimes I've gone longer distances. I love cats, but I've never had one. I've seen all the old John Wayne westerns..." She felt like she was rambling, but she kept going. "I have a birthmark on my chin that my dad tells me looks like a banana." She tilted her head to the ceiling and pointed it out. "Let's see, I'm a pretty fast reader. Sometimes I can finish a book in one night."

His mouth curled up on one side when she said that, but as soon as she reciprocated the almost-smile, he averted his eyes. A few minutes later the pizza came and Josie dished out a piece for each of them. Payton ate his slowly, while Josie inhaled hers, and grabbed a second piece before he'd even gotten through half of his first.

"What else?" she asked, thinking out loud. "Oh, I love the mountains. My best friend lives in Colorado, and I'm going to go visit her out there this summer. We haven't seen each other in a while."

Josie chattered on, trying to fill the silence that seemed to be swallowing them up. By the time they left, she was out of things to talk about, exhausting her list of random tidbits. They walked to the car in silence, and drove back to the Griers'. When she put her car in park, she turned to Payton.

"Same time next week?" she asked, not entirely sure what she would even have to say to him next week, having used up most of her conversation material tonight.

He shrugged.

"Okay, then. If you have homework, go ahead and bring it, too, if you need to."

Payton reached for the car door handle and turned it. Josie was about to say goodbye when he suddenly turned to look at her, holding her gaze for the longest he had all night.

"It doesn't look like a banana," he said, matter-of-factly. "It looks like California."

Josie's hand instinctively went to her chin, feeling the raised part of it under her fingers. Payton smiled, then shut the car door and walked inside the Griers' house. When she realized her hand was still on her face, she quickly pulled it away and put the car in reverse, backing out of the driveway. Every so often, though, her fingers went back to the crescent moon-shaped marking, affectionately feeling the spot that had finally gotten Payton Runnells to speak to her.

The next week, Josie brought Payton to her apartment. She'd put meat in the crock pot for sloppy joes, mixed some fruit together, and bought a few bags of chips. When they walked through the door, the whole place smelled like loose meat, making Josie's stomach growl.

"You can put your bag on the couch there," she said to Payton as she took her coat off. "I'll give you the short tour of my place."

Josie walked to the middle of the room and faced Payton, who still stood in the doorway, holding his backpack.

"This," she said, pointing to her right, "is the living room." She pointed to her left. "And this, over here, is the kitchen." She turned and did her best Vanna White impression. "This is the dining room," Josie said, realizing that this was all very obvious. "You probably knew all this when you first walked in, huh? Alright, this way." She walked a few steps past what she'd deemed the dining room and stopped, motioning for Payton to follow her. He did. "This is the bathroom," she said. Then, turning, she tapped on the door behind her, "and this is my bedroom. You won't need to go in there, but you'll probably want to know where the bathroom is. This place is huge, ya know?" She smiled in case he didn't realize she was joking. "Don't want you getting lost."

"You live here by yourself?" he asked as he looked around.

Josie nodded.

"Yep. Like I said, I've always wanted a cat, but just haven't gotten around to getting one. Do the Griers have any pets?"

"Nah," Payton said, turning back to the living room and sliding his bag off his shoulder. "Do you mind if I read?"

"Oh, no, that's fine. I need to check on dinner, anyway."

As he took out a book and settled onto the couch, Josie made herself busy in the kitchen. She got them each a glass of water in the retro, green-tinted Coca Cola glasses her dad had found one weekend antiquing. The glasses reminded her of an old diner, and she always had a bit of nostalgia when she used them, wondering what it would have been like to visit the diners and drive-ins of an older era. Those seemed like such simple times. Her dad loved watching reruns of the oldies, like "The Andy Griffith Show" and "Leave It to Beaver," and they would often stay up late watching back-to-back episodes together when she was a kid.

Josie stole glances at Payton while she opened the chip bags and stirred up the bowl of fresh-cut fruit. At first glance he seemed completely engrossed in his book, but Josie was pretty sure he was keeping an eye on her as she moved about the kitchen. He had yet to flip a page. She guessed it would have been hard to concentrate in the entirely new surroundings he now found himself in.

"Dinner's ready," she said, carrying their drinks to the table. "There are chips and fruit on the counter and you can make your own sandwich."

"What are we having?" Payton asked, putting down his book.

"Sloppy joes," she responded. "Okay, I admit it's really just hamburger meat mixed up with ketchup and mustard and a little bit of onion, but that's how my dad always made it, so I call it a sloppy joe, but technically it's probably not." She was rambling again. "There are pickles on the counter, too, if you want those."

"Sure," he picked up a plate and made a sandwich before heaping a big helping of fruit onto it and a few chips.

"So," Josie started as she made her own sandwich, "How about tonight you tell me a little about yourself?"

"What do you want to know?"

"Anything. Whatever you think I should know."

He stared at his plate, taking his sandwich in his hands and holding it in mid-air. "Alright. Well, I'm basically an orphan," He paused, not looking at Josie. Her heart hurt for him, but she didn't let it show. She wanted him to continue talking without feeling like she was pitying him. "I've got red hair like my mom. Everyone used to tell me how much I looked like her." When he took a bite of his sandwich, he chewed it quickly, and Josie was glad to see that he seemed to like it. Putting a few grapes in his mouth, he bit down on one that squirted grape juice out onto his chin. He absently wiped his sleeve across it to stop it from dripping. "My mom left last year. I don't know where she is or why she left—just didn't pick me up from school one day. Never had any pets. One of my foster families had a bunny, but it was a pretty boring pet if you ask me. Not many friends. I keep to myself mostly."

"You don't hang out with any kids at school?"

"Nah. A few weeks ago I got into some fights with a kid from my class. He kept harassing me about living with the Humphreys. They were my fosters before the Griers. I guess they go to the same church as this kid—Giovanni's his name—and his parents."

"How'd the fight start?"

Payton shrugged. "I was getting hassled by the teacher for not handing in an assignment. Giovanni started saying just awful stuff about how the Humphreys must not be doing their job and I'd probably be sent to a new home because of it. That they try to seem all righteous, but that it's all for show and they could give two shits about me. I don't know, it was probably true, but I wasn't going to let some asshole like Giovanni tell me that, like he knows anything about anything."

Josie chose to ignore the cussing for now. "What happened after?"

"Oh, we both got sent down to the office. They called Giovanni's parents, and he probably got his iPhone taken away for an hour or something. They called the Humphreys too, but no one answered, so after a while they just gave up. The Humphreys didn't have cell phones or an answering machine, and they'd just let the phone ring and ring sometimes. I mean if they were really busy and stuff. They had a lot of kids to look after, and I was one of the last to be placed with them. They must've realized it was too many. Since the Griers had just been approved as fosters, I got switched."

"The Griers seem to be a nice couple," Josie offered.

"Yeah, they're fine. Kind of old, though."

"Aw, they're not that old."

"Well, anyway, I haven't been there long enough to really know what they're like. Mrs. Grier—Mae, I mean—she's always hovering around, asking if I need anything. Sometimes I'll go walk outside just to get away for a little bit."

"In this weather?"

"Yeah, it's not that bad. I like to be outside."

"Certainly she's just worried about you."

Payton let out a skeptical laugh. "I think she just wants to make sure I don't steal anything."

Josie took a bite of her sandwich, before reaching for her glass. "I'm sure that's not it. Have you ever stolen anything before? I mean, would she have any reason to think that?"

"No," Payton said. "Anyway, they're nice enough."

Josie stood up to refill her drink. "Do you have any friends you still talk to from your old neighborhood?"

"Not really. Maybe one—Ira. He's probably the closest friend I've got. He lived next door to me and my mom. He was a few years older than me, but when my mom left and I had to move...." His voice trailed off.

"Could you call him?"

Payton shrugged. "Ira's not really the type to just sit around talking on the phone."

Josie tried another approach. "That's an interesting name for somebody your age—Ira."

"Yeah, he always hated it. It was his grandpa's name or something."

Josie thought of her own middle name, Louisa. Her dad had picked it after his own mother, who had passed away right before Josie was born. She'd always loved that it connected her to someone so important to her dad, and it made her a bit sad to think this Ira didn't feel the same.

"You done?"

Payton looked at his empty plate. "Yeah, thanks."

Josie reached across the table and picked up his plate, stacking it on hers and carrying them both back to the kitchen. Payton stood up and made his way back to the couch where he picked up his book and started reading again. Josie looked up from the sink long enough to see him steal a glance at her, then turned to clean up.

When she'd finished putting everything back in its proper place, she walked to her bedroom and grabbed her own book before taking a seat on the opposite end of the couch. She studied him over the top of her pages, watching as his eyes darted back and forth as he read. He'd opened up to her in a small way, and she was grateful for it. They were getting to know each other—feeling each other out. But Josie knew that talking wasn't everything. Sometimes it was enough just to be with someone, and show them that you wanted to be there too.

6.

JOSIE AND PAYTON SAW MORE OF EACH OTHER OVER THE next few weeks, usually on Wednesdays for dinner and sometimes again over the weekend. By the end of March, they'd gotten into a nice routine, and Josie was eager to introduce Payton to her dad. She had a feeling that they'd hit it off. So when he called to tell her he was planning to get the feeders out, she called Payton immediately.

"It's a McCray tradition. We clean them out every year right before spring." She could hear Payton breathing on the other line, but he didn't say anything. "Payton? Are you there? What do you think? Do you want to come with me?"

"Really, Josie? To clean bird feeders?"

"Yeah, it'll be fun."

"Uh, ok." He didn't sound convinced.

"I'll pick you up Saturday morning. And just to make it worth your while, I'll even bring donuts."

"Well in that case…"

"That's the spirit. I'll be there at 9."

Josie had stopped at Donut Top Café and picked up a few long johns, apple fritters and a French cruller (her personal favorite). Payton was waiting for her outside when she pulled up the driveway. As he opened the car door, she noticed Mrs. Grier standing in the doorway and waved to her. She waved back before heading back into the house.

"When do you need to be back?" Josie asked, handing him the sack of donuts as he slid into the seat beside her.

"Eh, anytime is fine. I told Mae I'd call if it was going to be after lunch."

"Good."

Payton reached in and grabbed a maple long john out of the bag, getting the icing on his fingers. "Did you get napkins, too?"

"In the glove box."

"Thanks," he said before taking a big bite. "The Griers only had some corn flakes in the cupboard this morning, so I was hoping you wouldn't let me down."

"I don't joke around about donuts," Josie said, motioning for the bag and taking out the cruller. "I'm going to need one of those, too."

"So, what's the big deal with the bird feeders?" Payton asked as he passed a napkin to Josie.

"You know, I can't really tell you. It's just something my dad and I have always done together." As Josie drove out of town towards Druid Falls, she licked her lips to get the glazed icing off, enjoying the savory treat. "Even when I went off to college, I'd make sure to come back whatever weekend he was going to get them out."

Payton finished off his long john and reached in for another. "Can I have this one, too?"

Josie nodded. "Just save me one of the fritters. Oh, and don't tell my dad I bribed you with sugar to get you to come."

Payton laughed. "I probably would have come anyway. What else would I be doing?"

"True," Josie joked, then immediately felt bad about it. But when she turned to look at Payton, he was still smiling, unaffected.

"The snow's finally melting," Josie said after they'd been driving a while.

"About time. Hey, did I tell you the Griers are getting me a new bike so I can ride to school the rest of the year?"

"No," Josie said, surprised. "That's nice of them."

"Yeah, I'm stoked," he said. "Plus, the ride to school is awkward sometimes. Mae usually takes me, but she doesn't really talk and she won't turn on the radio."

"Maybe she's just not a morning person."

"Maybe."

"I'm sure that she and Mr. Grier are just trying to give you space."

He was silent, looking out the window as they passed through the countryside. The once-snowy soybean and corn fields stood derelict, waiting for their moment of functionality. Farmers were surely preparing to till and ready them for planting.

"I know," he said, finally.

It hit Josie that maybe Payton didn't want to get close to the Griers. He had, after all, been bounced from one foster home to the next.

Then, as if he had read her mind, he asked, "Do you think if they don't like me, or I get moved again, that we would still see each other?"

"I'd hope so," she said. "But I wouldn't worry about that. You'd have to move pretty far to get rid of me."

"Yeah, I thought so." He put his head back, resting it on the seat headrest, the corners of his mouth upturned in a smile.

"You made it," Josie's dad was already outside when they pulled in.

"Dad," Josie said as she got out of the car. He wrapped his arms around her, squeezing her tightly in a massive bear hug. When he finally let go, her eyes moved to Payton. Her father followed her gaze, watching as the boy climbed out of the car and slammed the car door shut. "This is Payton," she said as her dad moved around to the other side of the car.

"Nice to meet you, Payton. I'm John McCray. Been wondering when Jo was going to bring you around."

Payton smiled, and Josie watched as her dad put an arm around the boy, welcoming him.

"So, how'd she get you to agree to help clean out bird feeders today? Doesn't seem like the type of thing a young lad like you would be keen to do on a Saturday morning." Before Payton could answer, her dad's eyes lit up and he looked at Josie. "It couldn't have something to do with donuts, could it?"

"Me?" Josie said, feigning disbelief and putting a hand on her chest dramatically. "Never!"

"Payton, my boy, one thing you'll need to beware of hanging out with this one. Her love of donuts is legendary. She once ate seven in one sitting. One after the other. And, they were big, too! The girl didn't even bat an eye. Just inhaled them like it was nothing."

"What?" Payton asked, looking at Josie in surprise.

"I won't deny it. Let's just say that it was very ill-advised and I crashed like crazy later that day."

"You bet she did!"

"Dad, c'mon, it was a one-time thing," she said. Then, turning to Payton she added, "Sugar is bad. This is a do as I say, not as I do type of situation."

Payton laughed, shaking his head.

"Now that you two are all hopped up on sugar, let's get to the exciting stuff!" Josie's dad said, rubbing his hands together in anticipation.

"I'm ready," Payton said.

"Lead the way," Josie added, smiling at her dad.

The feeders were all out and spread across the deck. A few buckets with soapy water were also ready to go. Payton went over and picked up one of the many finch feeders, running his fingers over every piece of it, inspecting it in a way only a curious young boy could.

"Man, there are a lot of feeders here," he said.

"Yeah, we don't always put all of them out, but we usually clean them all and then decide which ones we'll use for the summer," Josie said as she pulled out the suet feeders. "Now these here are my favorites. Not the most aesthetically pleasing by any means, but the jays love 'em."

"Blue jays?" Payton asked.

"Yeah, they're aggressive birds, but I didn't know that as a little girl. All I knew was that they were blue, and looked like just about the prettiest birds I'd ever seen. It always seemed so special to spot one."

"Oh yeah," Josie's dad said as he took a seat on one of the old white wrought iron patio chairs. The set of chairs and table were reminiscent of other mid-century designs, simplistic and functional. A few feeders were sitting on the table, and Josie watched as her dad took one in his hand, beginning to dust it off. "Jo would look for them all the time. And, she probably won't admit it now, but she loved it when they'd swoop down on the smaller birds. She'd giggle and cheer 'em on, but eventually some of the bigger ones started swooping down on ol' Tooley, and we finally had to chase those off."

"Poor, Tooley. He was the cat that lived next door," she added, to Payton. "Remember that awful Rita Jenkins, Dad? She'd see us filling up the feeders and she'd come outside and grab Tooley and just stand in her yard, petting him and staring us down. You'd finally holler over at her, asking if she wanted to help us put the food out and she'd look down at the poor cat she was just about strangling and say "C'mon, Tooley baby. Let's go inside where it's safe." Oh, she had it out for you, Dad. I'm sure she thought we were putting bird food out just to annoy her!"

"Well, Jo, you always wanted to put the peanuts out for the jays and squirrels. That's what really got her going. She knew that meant she'd have to keep that dang cat inside. Ah, anyway, she was no harm."

"Does she still live there?" Payton asked.

"Her daughter moved to Minneapolis after college, got married, started a family. Rita stayed a few years, but she wanted to be around those grandbabies, so she and her husband moved out there just about five years ago. And 'ol Tooley was gone a few years before that."

"Dad doesn't like the new occupants much," Josie said, winking at Payton.

"Now, now. It's not that I don't like them. I just don't see them. People these days just don't come outside. Everybody's holed up in their houses, keeping to themselves. I don't understand it. When I was your age, Payton, we spent every second outside that we could and we wouldn't come in until our mothers threatened to tan our hides. Nowadays everybody's staring at their phone or texting their friend down the street instead of getting off their rumps and livin' life."

Payton laughed. "I like being outside, too."

"Jo, help Payton soak that finch feeder, there."

Josie handed the feeder to Payton and moved a sudsy bucket closer to him. "Just let that one soak for about five minutes, then grab that rag." She motioned to the yellow rag on the bench next to him. "And wipe off all the grime. Once you've wiped it clean, we'll put it in one of those buckets on the steps for 10 minutes or so. There's bleach in those."

"We'll let them dry overnight," her dad added. "Supposed to have clear skies, I think."

Payton slipped the feeder into the water, watching as it filled each of the holes and rose to the top, causing it to sink into the bucket. Josie did the same with the suet feeder sitting between them. She put her hand over her eyes, shielding them from the sun, and looked out over the backyard. Waiting for the feeders to soak had always proved difficult for Josie, and, as a girl, she found herself constantly distracted by the awakening bugs and animals that wanted to welcome spring—but today she felt peaceful. The sun was warm on her face, while the cool breeze, one of the last reminders of winter, perked up her senses.

A short time later Payton pulled his feeder from the bucket, rubbing off the scum with the yellow washcloth. "Are these up all winter, too?" he asked.

"Some of them are," Josie heard her dad say. He was standing near the edge of the deck where six or seven small feeders lay on the floorboards, scrutinizing them to determine which ones might need repair. "Payton, come on over here a minute."

He set his feeder down and joined Josie's dad on the other side of the deck. "This feeder is my favorite." Josie knew which one it was without even looking. She'd made it herself in shop class, begging the teacher to deviate from the regular assignment to do it. It was a painted wood feeder with a compartment that held up to five pounds of bird seed. Josie had painted it blue and white, then, by freehand, she'd painted a few birds on the hinged roof of the feeder.

"Can you believe Jo made this?" he asked, setting it on the railing of the deck as if it was a prestigious award that needed to be displayed.

"That's awesome, Josie," Payton said. Then, turning to Josie, he asked, "So you paint, too?"

"Oh, no," Josie said. "That's about the only thing I've ever painted well. I've tried to paint since and nothing turns out. It was a total fluke that the feeder turned out as good as it did."

Using old *National Geographic* magazines her dad had left sitting out, she'd copied the birds as best she could—one jay, a hummingbird and a cardinal. She'd picked birds that were distinct in coloring, birds that she loved to see at the feeders. Josie still remembered the absolute precision with which she'd painted, slowly creating feathers, wings and beaks.

"It's the best gift I've ever gotten," John said, smiling.

"How about a run?" Josie asked later after they'd made their way back to Montpier. They were sitting in Josie's car, in front of the Griers' house.

"Right now?"

"Why not?"

"Don't you have other stuff to do today?"

Josie shook her head. "Not really. I mean, I've always got schoolwork, but I've got tonight and tomorrow to do some."

"You do schoolwork on the weekends?"

"Yeah, it's not an 8-5 job."

"What about plans? Don't you have a date to get ready for or, I don't know, like friends to see or something?"

"Nope."

"Well," he rubbed his cheek, mulling this over. "I don't have any shoes to wear."

"You don't have sneakers?"

"I do. It's just," he looked at Josie, obviously displeased. "They're not for running. They're old."

"We're not going to run 10 miles, you know. Just a short run. You can get a feel for whether or not you like it and maybe it will help you decide if you want to sign up for a race with me."

He ran a hand through his hair, which was longer now than it had been when they'd first met. "Yeah, alright," he said, finally.

"I've got clothes with me. You think Mrs. Grier will mind if I change inside?"

"I doubt it."

Josie popped the trunk and grabbed her extra bag of clothes out of it. She always had extra running gear in her car, and today she was especially glad for it.

A few minutes later, she and Payton were sitting on the curb in front of the Griers' house as Payton tied his shoelaces, tucking them in as Josie had done. They'd been in Druid Falls for most of the day, and now the sun was low in the sky.

"Okay, first we'll do a little warm-up run around the block. Then we'll come back here and stretch out before we take off."

Payton nodded. He'd put a hat on at Josie's suggestion to keep his hair from flopping around.

"Have you ever run before?" Josie asked.

"Does gym class count?"

"What'd you do? A mile?"

"Yeah, twice a year. Timed."

"Then, yes, that counts. Of course it counts." Josie tightened her ponytail, then looked at Payton. "Ready?"

"I guess."

It was a leisurely start, which Josie expected. She slowed up her steps to match his after feeling out his pace during their warm-up. She stole glances at him as they ran, trying her best to be discreet.

"So, how much faster do you usually go?"

"Not much," she said. Payton shot her a look. "Honest!"

"Do you run with music?"

"Usually."

"You didn't bring it with you?"

"Nah," she said, pulling her arm in front of her, stretching out her triceps. "I don't listen when I've got a running buddy."

"A running buddy?"

She laughed. "Yeah, that's what we are. Running buddies."

"Is that what all runners call it?"

"Just the cool ones," she said.

They ran up through the main part of town, weaving through streets Josie was less familiar with. The new terrain excited her, and she realized she needed to get out of her routine and explore other routes. This unforeseen perk was just one of the benefits to running with Payton. She made a mental note to thank Ben later for the idea.

"Ready to head back?" she asked as Payton slowed beside her.

"Can we stop a minute?" he asked.

She nodded and turned back to him. He was staring across the street, lost in thought. "Is that your old school?" she asked.

He didn't say anything, and Josie realized he was worlds away from her. Squinting his eyes, he raised his hand to shield them from the glare of the sun. His brow wrinkled in consternation. She reached out, placing her hand on his shoulder and he startled at the touch.

"You okay?"

"Uh, yeah," he said, failing to convince her. "Let's head back, if that's alright."

"Sure," she said.

"Sorry," he murmured as they began jogging back.

"No problem..." she said, trying to sound casual.

He looked up at her. "I didn't realize we'd run this far." It was an attempt to change the subject, she knew. Something had spooked him, but she didn't want it to be what he remembered about this run, so she kept the mood light.

"Didn't know you had it in you, did you?"

He smiled and shook his head, morphing back into the carefree kid who'd started out on this run. "No," he said. "I really didn't."

Josie picked up her bottle of water and took a long sip, feeling the coolness make its way down her throat. She, Claire and Thresia had been sitting in Thresia's classroom for more than an hour now, tossing around ideas for their Dr. Seuss unit, before Thresia reminded them that they needed to move on to discuss ideas for a science unit on matter.

"Obviously the Alka-Seltzer experiment should be included, but what else are you guys planning to do?" Claire asked, thumbing through some of the print-outs in front of her.

"What about something with movement? When I was student teaching, my cooperating teacher did this exercise where the kids would all bunch up really close together so they wouldn't be able to move—a solid," Josie said, clasping her hands together to mimic the action. "Then all the kids take a step away from each other. They have more room to move—

they're a liquid. Then they spread out all over the room so they have as much space as possible—they're a gas. The kids seemed to understand everything that way."

"We've done something similar in the past," Thresia said. "It worked well."

"Are you guys hoping to finish this unit up before spring break?" Claire asked.

"I am," Josie said, wiggling her toes under the table. "Don't you think? We've still got units on energy and magnets to do before the simple machines intro."

"I am, too, but I'm not sure it will be possible." Thresia let out a deep sigh. "A few of mine are lagging behind right now. I know the third grade team doesn't expect us to do the simple machines intro if we can't fit it in. They do the bulk of that one. Let's play these next few weeks by ear, and then we can decide if we'll push through with the simple machines the last week of school."

"Sounds good to me," Claire said, jotting down some notes.

"Now, on to more important things," Thresia said, leaning back in her chair.

Josie put down her pen and stretched her arms out in front of her, trying not to yawn, but failing and letting her breath out slowly. Thresia's eyes were on both of them, and her face looked calm and composed considering all the planning they had just done.

"After a long talk with Bill—quite a long talk, actually, that's lasted a few months," she paused, rubbing her fingers back and forth on the soft surface of the oak table where they sat. "I've decided that this is going to be my last year here."

"Oh, Thresia," Claire said, reaching out for Thresia's hands and squeezing them tightly, "I'm ecstatic for you—well, you and Bill. You'll finally be retired together."

While Claire was immediately congratulatory, Josie was stunned silent. She knew Thresia could have retired at any time, but for some reason, she hadn't thought it would be so

THE BLUE JAY

soon. She smiled the most genuine smile she could muster, and finally forced some words out. "We will really miss you."

"I haven't checked out, yet, ladies," Thresia's tone was lighthearted, but her eyes darted back and forth from Josie to Claire. "You're stuck with me for another few months. I just wanted you to be the first at Montpier to know."

"A hectic morning of meetings, a lengthy afternoon of curriculum planning and now news that our luminary is leaving," Claire said, shaking her head. "This professional development day has turned from bad to worse." She meant it figuratively, but Josie could have agreed to it in a more literal sense.

"What do you and Bill plan to do first?" Josie asked, surprised at how upset she felt. She wanted to be happy for Thresia. And she was happy, but not as overjoyed as she should be.

"You know, I'm not sure. He's been talking about Hawaii for the last few years. We've never been and I know people love vacationing there. I just don't know if it's for me."

"Oh, it's for you," Claire said. "Hawaii is for everyone."

Thresia laughed. "I suppose, but I think I'd much rather head to Yosemite and spend a few weeks doing some of their nature and history programs."

"Why doesn't that surprise me?" Josie said, smiling. "Well, whatever you decide will be amazing."

"Thank you ladies," she said, looking at them both with enough emotion behind her eyes that Josie almost started crying right there. "I admit I was nervous to tell you. Claire, working with you has been wonderful. You're the most positive person I know. And, Josie, it has been so rewarding to watch you dive into teaching this year with so much gusto. I'll tell you, it restores my faith in the next generation of teachers—it does."

"I suppose it was going to happen sooner or later," Claire said. "You've already stayed on many more years than I plan to." She winked at Josie, who melodramatically put her hand to her chest, opening her mouth wide as in shock.

"That better not be true," she said, in mock horror, realizing she was probably only partially joking.

Their laughter slowly subsided as she and Claire gathered their things to return their own rooms. While they had spent a large part of the day in the throes of planning, the time had gone fast. It usually did—the three of them so in tune with each other they could fly through their work without it even feeling like work. How many more hours would they spend together like this before the end of the year—before someone new was sitting in Thresia's spot? Josie knew that the world didn't stop when something went wrong. She had enough experience to know better. But it didn't stop her from wishing it would when something was going so right.

Josie picked up her 14-pound ball, adjusted her fingers in the holes and walked up the bowling lane. She found her mark, swung her arm and released. The ball spun towards the pins, crashing into the center one, creating a domino effect until all of the pins had been pushed down.

"And that's how you do it," Josie said, clapping her hands together as she took a seat next to Payton.

"Beginner's luck," he said. This was their second game and Josie had smoked him in the last one, too.

"Just because you're younger than me, doesn't mean I'm going to let you win. You've got to work for it."

Payton rolled his eyes. "Whatever," he mumbled, picking up his own ball and walking up the lane. He paused, finding his stance, swung back and watched the ball roll down the lane. Two pins were left standing. He turned away, sulking. "Why did I agree to this again?"

"Because we haven't been to a group event yet," Josie said, looking around at her fellow mentors and their matches across the bowling alley. "And bowling is fun!"

"I guess."

The bowling alley was crowded with kids. Katherine was standing on one end, bowling with six kids who didn't have mentors. Oliver was standing near the entrance, watching everyone, but also keeping an eye out for any late arrivals. Josie and Payton had been one of the last few to arrive, ending up with a lane all to themselves.

"How many games do we have to play?" Payton asked after he'd bowled his second round, missing the still-standing pins.

"You mean get to play, right?" Josie teased. "C'mon, it's raining out. What else are we going to do today?"

"I don't know. I'm in the middle of my book right now. I could be finishing it."

"As much as I love the fact that you read so much, it's important to get out of your head once in a while. You never know who you might meet or what you might learn."

Payton shrugged. This was definitely out of his comfort zone. But, it wasn't just the loud atmosphere and crazy kids running wild about the place that made Payton look like a fish out of water. While those things were more than enough to overstimulate the senses, Josie had noticed it was something else that had caused Payton's attitude to go from eager participant to disinterested observer. A few minutes into their first game, a woman had walked over and started punching names into the scoring computer. Seconds later, a young boy emerged from the bathroom, his eyes full of excitement. "Where's my ball, Mom?" he'd asked, and she'd directed him to the balls lined up against the wall. He'd gone over to pick one out, bouncing the whole way, while his mother had watched, grinning like a Cheshire cat.

As soon as Payton had seen this scene play out, his shoulders had slumped a little, and he'd lost all interest in the game.

"Payton!" Josie turned, seeing Katherine, with her hands on her hips, feigning anger. "What are you doing? Letting Josie win?"

"Nah," he said. Then, nodding in her direction, he added, "Josie doesn't believe in letting people win."

"A girl after my own heart," Katherine said, smiling at Josie.

"I'm going to get a snack," Payton said, before making his way to the concession booth.

"Do you need some money?" Josie asked, her eyes darting around looking for her purse. She needed to do a better job of keeping tabs on her stuff, she realized when she finally spotted it hidden under a nearby table where she had changed into her bowling shoes. But Payton had already pulled out a wad of cash and headed for the food line.

"So, how's it going?" Katherine asked. She looked concerned, probably because this was the first My Mentor & Me outing she and Payton had been to, and to Katherine, it probably wasn't looking too good.

"It's actually going really well. I know this is our first monthly event. I had wanted to try and get to last month's, but we were really still getting to know each other..."

Katherine held up a hand. "Don't apologize for that. It's not a requirement, although we do love to see all the kids and mentors, too. However you choose to spend time together is up to you and Payton."

"Oh," Josie said. She hadn't realized that. "Well, for the most part things have been going great. We're starting to run together. I think we may even sign up for a race sometime this summer."

"That's awesome."

"Yeah, you know the first few times we got together were a little awkward, but I think he is starting to open up a bit."

Katherine nodded. "Well, I'm glad you both made it today." She paused, watching as Payton paid at the counter. "You know, the first weekend in September we're putting on our first road race. It's the Miles for Mentors 5K, and the mentees are welcome to run, too. Payton would probably do fine, especially if you're already running with him."

"That would be perfect. I'm glad you told me. I've been looking online for some end-of-summer races, but I haven't found one to get really excited about."

"Great," Katherine said.

Suddenly, Josie felt a hand on her shoulder. "Josie," the voice behind her said. "How's it going?"

She turned to see Oliver, followed closely by an older gentleman and a young boy. "Hi, Oliver. It's good to see you again."

"I was just telling Josie about our 5K in September. She and Payton have been running together."

Oliver looked impressed. His eyes moved in Payton's direction, who was returning to his seat carrying a cup and several Laffy Taffys. "Josie turning you into a runner?" he asked Payton.

"Yeah," Payton said, tugging on the plastic wrapper of the candy.

Oliver didn't wait for him to say more. "I thought since you two weren't too far into your second game that you wouldn't mind if Ray and Kaleb here joined you?" He motioned to the two figures standing next to him.

"Of course not," Josie said, smiling in their direction.

"Great," Oliver said. "I'll have them reset your game."

Josie nodded as Katherine gave her a little wave and Oliver headed off to talk with the employee on duty.

"Ray Nelsen," the man said, reaching out his hand. Josie took it, feeling his tight grip as her hand moved up and down. "This here's Kaleb." He pointed to the young boy beside him.

"I'm Josie," she said, then motioned in Payton's direction, introducing him, too.

"Nice to meet you, Josie," he said. "Thanks for letting us butt in on your game."

"It's no problem. We'd really just started again." Josie watched as Payton chewed on his candy, eyeing Kaleb. She couldn't tell for sure, but he looked a little annoyed to have these two added to their lane.

Once Josie had entered everyone's names, they started to bowl. First Ray, then Kaleb, followed by Payton, then Josie. Ray turned out to be a bowling shark, which turned Payton's frown around to finally see Josie losing. He had loosened up considerably by the third frame, and was no longer distracted by the woman and her son in the lane next to them.

"You've got to kind of turn your wrist," he was explaining to Kaleb, who looked up in awe at Payton. He was probably six or seven years old, just about the same age gap between Josie and Mia. "Like this. And look down at the arrows on the floor." He pointed down the lane.

Kaleb nodded, listening intently.

"Your boy there is quite a lad," Ray said as they watched the two boys. Payton picked up Kaleb's ball, handing it to him as he gave him more tips.

"He's a good kid," Josie agreed.

"Have you been mentoring long?"

"Not long. Just a few months."

Ray must have been about the same age as her dad, but he had a lot more gray hair, and the fine lines around his eyes and mouth gave him a weathered look that made Josie wonder if he had spent a lot of his time working outside.

"What about you?" she asked.

"Just over a year. Kaleb's got two younger brothers, so sometimes I bring them along, too. I think he feels bad for them when we leave. He helps take care of them."

"What do you mean?" Josie asked, wondering how a child as young as Kaleb could help out much with two younger siblings.

"Well, they live with their mom, but she's in and out a lot. She calls me all the time to see if I can take the kids. I have a few times, but I've got a job, too, as a construction foreman."

"Of course," Josie said, surprised she hadn't thought of parents thinking a mentor could be a free babysitter. "Payton's with a foster family."

"Ah," he said, and she wondered if he thought that might be a better situation.

"A strike!" Kaleb yelled. Josie turned just in time to see the final pin fall. Payton was beaming.

The Blue Jay

"Looks like you found yourself quite a coach there," Ray said.

Kaleb ran over to Ray and climbed up beside him, but his eyes stayed on Payton, who had gone from unknown partner to revered role model in an instant.

The rest of the game went quickly. Ray won, but he tried not to make a big fuss about it, showing Josie a much more admirable way to win. She wasn't sure he had even wanted to win, but the ball just kept knocking pins down, giving him strikes and spares again and again. Josie's own competitiveness disappeared as she really began to enjoy the company she was in, watching Payton take Kaleb under his wing, cracking him up with silly jokes and patting him on the back after his frames.

As they switched back into their street shoes, Ray thanked Josie again. "Maybe we'll see you guys next month." Josie looked over at Payton, who shrugged.

"That would be great," Josie said.

"Take care, you two," he replied. Kaleb waved at Payton, then followed Ray past the crowded entryway and out the door.

"Ready to go?" Josie asked as she finished tying her shoes. Payton nodded and the two started to make their way to the exit when she heard a voice call out Payton's name. Turning, she saw an older boy with shoulder-length blonde hair. He was smiling, but it wasn't a genuine smile. It was more of a smirk than a smile. It reminded Josie of the kind of grin you'd see on a race opponent's face after you tripped and fell a few feet from the finish line, leaving the win open for the taking. It left a bad taste in Josie's mouth.

"Hey, man," the older kid said, high-fiving Payton and pulling him into one of those tough-guy hugs with a hard pat on the back. He was older than Payton. Josie figured he must've been around 15 or 16.

"Ira," Payton said, looking surprised. "What are you doing here?"

"Just hangin' with the guys," he said. Then he nodded to Josie. "Who's the old lady?"

Okay, Josie thought, she officially did not like this kid.

"Oh, this is Josie," Payton said, moving his body between them almost protectively.

Josie smiled through gritted teeth, but Ira had already turned his attention back to Payton.

"So, hey, man, where have you been? Haven't seen you around since...I don't even know. Heard your Mom left. Is that true?"

"Yeah," Payton said, looking down at his feet.

"Damn, that's rough," Ira said. He was so sympathetic that he whipped out his phone, tapped the screen, and only looked up again when one of his buddies punched him in the side of the arm. "Look, we gotta go, but call me sometime. You got my number, right?"

Payton nodded.

Ira stepped around him, followed by his entourage, and then looked back at Josie with a raised eyebrow, grinning like a bank robber going over his score. What was with this kid?

"See you around, Payton."

Payton watched him go, his head cocked to the side as if he wasn't sure what had just happened.

"See you."

"So that's the guy you consider your one friend?" Josie asked as they climbed into her car moments later.

Payton shrugged.

"I don't know. I haven't seen him in a long time," he said.

"I can see why."

"He's not that bad. I mean, when he's not with all those guys." Payton looked out the window, and Josie began the drive home. Payton might think Ira wasn't so bad, but Josie, well, she wasn't so sure.

7.

"Thanks for meeting us here," Mrs. Grier said, putting her arm around Josie's shoulders. They were standing outside Southwoods Elementary and Josie had no idea why.

Mr. Grier appeared from inside, waving them in. "They're ready to see us," he said, then disappeared back inside. Josie's stomach was in knots, wondering what could possibly have happened that was bad enough for this type of meeting.

All Mrs. Grier had told her on the phone was that Payton had gotten into trouble and they were heading up to the school. "I want him to have an ally there, and I don't know if he sees us that way," she had said. Luckily, it was the end of the day and Thresia had offered to cover her class after they'd come back from art. It was only 20 minutes and making sure all her students got home, so Josie didn't feel too terrible getting permission to take off early.

"Mr. and Mrs. Grier," a man said as they entered the front office. He reached out to shake their hands. "I'm sorry we have to meet under these circumstances."

"So are we," Mr. Grier said, his voice more pained than it was upset. "This is Payton's mentor, Josie." He nodded in her direction and she stepped forward to shake the principal's hand.

"Josie," he said, taking her hand. "I'm David Sawyers, the vice principal here at Southwoods." Then, he opened the door behind him and motioned for them to follow him into his personal office. As they entered, her eyes immediately went to Payton. He was sitting in a chair on the far side of the room, his head in his hands.

The Grier's took the seats in front of Principal Sawyers' desk, and Josie made her way to the seat next to Payton. He didn't look up, and she guessed he didn't know she was going to be there.

"Thank you all for coming in today," Principal Sawyers said as he sat down, facing the Griers. "First off, I want you to know that we care deeply about the academic success of our students. We also know that the potential for academic success cannot be reached if students aren't equipped to deal with their adversities, and we know that not all students have the support to do so." He took a breath. "Because Payton's situation is ever-changing, we realize school may be difficult for him. He's a very smart boy, who, at this time, we feel is unable to meet his full potential."

Josie looked from the principal to Payton, who was still disengaged. She put a hand on his back and he lifted his head, realizing for the first time that she was there. She mouthed the word hi, and he gave her a half-smile and mouthed it back.

"Today, Payton and one of our other students got into a heated argument as they were walking back to their classroom," Principal Sawyers continued. "His teacher, Ms. Eppley, asked them both to come down to the office, but only the other student arrived. We had two of our office workers looking for Payton for quite some time, finally finding him outside the school, a few yards away from the front entrance."

Mrs. Grier, a look of concern on her face, shot a glance at Payton.

"What kind of argument was it?" Mr. Grier asked. He rubbed at his right eyebrow.

"It wasn't physical. Just two boys exchanging unpleasant remarks. Neither would fess up to what the fight was about, and it doesn't seem that the other students were really paying attention to it before Ms. Eppley got involved. Perhaps Payton will

THE BLUE JAY

tell you about it later." He turned towards Payton then. "I hope he does."

Payton looked down at his shoes, embarrassed. Suddenly, a bell rang and hundreds of voices filled the hallways outside. School was being let out and you could feel the excitement coming from under the door.

"It's not the argument that I'm worried about, though. It— well, we can't have our students leaving the building, and this isn't a first-time occurrence. The other being after an outdoor science activity. The rest of the class went back inside, but Payton stayed outside. His teacher finally realized he hadn't come back in a few minutes later. It was something we dealt with, at the time, with his previous foster parents, and we thought a lunch detention would suffice as a punishment if he did it again."

Mrs. Grier nodded. "Of course."

"Payton's aware that should he leave the building again during school hours, he will have to serve an afternoon of in-school suspension."

"That's a perfectly acceptable punishment." Mr. Grier offered.

Principal Sawyers took his glasses off and crossed his arms on his desk.

"Look, I understand that a lot has gone on with Payton's home life recently. I can only imagine what he's gone through, and is still going through. We just need to keep our students safe." He spoke with great tenderness, and Josie could feel the affection he had for his students and for his school.

"Well, thank you for bringing this incident to our attention," Mrs. Grier said. She began to stand and smooth out the wrinkles from her gray pencil skirt.

"Thank you all for coming in today," he replied. Then, he turned his focus to the boy at the center of their discussion. "Let's move forward now and put this behind us. You choose what you want your path to be, Payton."

Once they were back outside, Josie offered to drive Payton home. They watched as the Griers pulled out of the parking lot. Josie took a seat on the concrete steps leading up to the entrance.

"I guess you want to know what happened," was all Payton said.

Josie patted the step she was sitting on, hoping he would sit down beside her. He did.

"Do you want to tell me?" she asked.

He shrugged.

"Payton, I understand the need to be alone. Sometimes I need my own space, too. I just have to hold out until I'm done teaching for the day." She offered a friendly smile, but he didn't look at her.

"It wasn't that," he said, finally. "I mean, I didn't need to be alone. It's just, the first time I stayed outside I just got lost in my thoughts. I didn't even realize everyone else had gone inside. I was watching the cars pass on the street. Looking in each one." He picked up a small rock and flicked it out into the patch of grass between them and the parking lot. "And this time, I was just angry. I went outside because I wanted to pretend she was coming to get me."

"You think she'll come for you?"

He shook his head. "No, not here, anyway. I didn't even go to this school before. Sometimes, I just like to pretend she will."

Josie put her arm around him, and he leaned into her, resting his head on her shoulder. It was comforting to see him relax with her. She was beginning to feel like she belonged here with him, that she fit into his life somehow.

"Sometimes pretending is all we've got," she said. "No harm in that."

He lifted his head after a moment. "The argument was stupid. This kid—Mick—he tripped me, and I told him to knock it off. He told me to bugger off, and I said why don't you make me? Then he said I'm not fighting no homeless bum. He started laughing like it was the funniest thing he'd ever heard. I yelled at him, calling him a jackass and that's when Ms. Eppley heard us."

"And jackass was the best you came up with?"

Payton looked up, surprised, then smiled. She winked at him, then stood up, brushing the dirt from her dress pants.

"I'm glad you came today," he said, watching her.

"Me too."

He startled Josie with his next words. "Do you ever feel like you're waiting for something more?"

"Like what?"

"I don't know. I feel sometimes like something's supposed to happen—something big or important." A breeze rustled through the trees nearby, causing Josie to look up to the sky. This time of year always made her want to sprawl out in the grass and watch the clouds, breathing in the air of the impending summer. "But then it never does, and I'm still left waiting," he said.

"That sounds disappointing." But she realized that she often felt the same. She looked over her shoulder at Payton who met her eyes. He looked miserable.

"It is," he said.

"What size are those?" Josie asked, checking her watch.

"These are a size six," the salesman responded, slipping one onto Payton's left foot. The shoes were royal blue, black and white, and Josie hoped they would keep Payton excited about the upcoming Miles for Mentors race. Once both shoes were on and tied, Payton jumped up from his seat. "Go ahead and run down that hallway, and get a feel for them."

Payton took off. Josie wasn't sure if it was the shoe itself that had him running with an extra bounce in his step, or just the fact that he was getting something new today. He'd commented on the fact that it'd been some time since he'd gotten anything new. Of course it would have been, but Josie found herself forgetting he was a foster kid. He rarely spoke about the things he didn't have, and it made this moment even more special.

"How do they feel?" Josie asked, crossing her arms in front of her as she watched Payton return from the hallway.

"They feel awesome."

The salesman, who had wandered away to help another customer, made his way back over. "Got enough room in there?" He bent down and felt for Payton's big toe.

"Yeah," Payton said, watching him. "There's quite a bit of space there."

"Well, you want a little space because when you run, your feet swell, so you want to give them room to do that. But, is it too much?"

"Nah, I don't think so." He wiggled his toes.

"So, what do you think? Are you sold on these or do you want to try some others?"

"I like these," Payton said. "I mean, if they aren't too much."

Josie put her hands on her hips. "You, Mr., are not going to worry about that today, and neither am I. This is your first big race, and we've got to break these shoes in before then." She turned to the salesman. "We'll take 'em."

Payton started to unlace the shoes to put them back in the box, but Josie stopped him.

"Just wear them out." She picked up his old ones and held them up. "You want to keep these?" One had a hole in the heel and the other was so worn out that any cushioning and support it had had to begin with was completely gone. She barely waited for Payton's response before she turned and threw them in the trash bin behind the checkout counter. "No turning back now," she said.

Once they were outside the running store, Payton took off down the sidewalk. "How do they look?" he yelled over his shoulder.

"They look fast," Josie said once he'd turned to run back towards her.

"Good."

"So, what now?" They were seated back in her car, and Josie adjusted her sunglasses. "I need a snack. You hungry?"

"Always."

"What sounds good?"

"I don't know. How about something spicy?"

"Okay. Like fajita-spicy or Thai-food spicy?"

"Thai food? What's that?"

Josie's mouth gaped wide open. "Are you joking? Please tell me you're joking."

"I'm not joking. What's Thai food?"

"Only the most delicious food you could ever eat!"

Payton laughed. "Even better than donuts?"

Josie scowled, starting up the car. "Payton Runnells. You are about to have your mind blown—or, more accurately, your taste buds blown."

"That doesn't sound like something I would want."

It didn't, did it? "Okay, what I mean is, you are going to love it. You like spicy food, just like I do." She pulled her glasses down to look him in the eye, so he'd know she was serious. "And Thai food is the best kind of spicy because it's also got a little bit of sweet thrown in."

"Okay, I'll try it."

Josie pushed her sunglasses back up as she backed out of the parking spot. "That's all I ask."

"Tyler, let's get going. The rest of the class is waiting." Josie stood by the entrance to her classroom, the students lined up in front of her, ready to walk out to their parents.

"But, Miss McCray, I'm going to miss you so much," he said, crossing his arms in front of his chest.

Josie smiled. Sometimes it was the most rambunctious students that stole your heart, and Tyler had definitely done that.

"Yes, but if you never leave, you'll never get to enjoy your summer break. Won't you miss swimming and going to the park, too?"

"My mom's making me go to science camp!" He made a face like he'd just told her he was going to be spending the summer detasseling corn or picking up trash along the highway.

"That sounds amazing," Josie said. "Then, you'll definitely be ready for third grade."

"I'll be ready for third grade, too." Hattie, one of the smallest in the class, was standing at the front of the line and waved her hand at Josie to make sure she knew she didn't want to be left behind.

"Luckily, you all are ready for third grade." Josie looked down at all the faces in front of her. They gleamed with excitement at the thought of moving on to third grade.

"But I will be especially because I'm going to science camp," Tyler told them, obviously rethinking his stance on the whole science camp thing.

"I want to go to science camp, too." Faye said.

"Well, you let your mom know, and maybe she can talk to Tyler's mom and find out which camp it is." Josie clapped her hands, hushing the students. "Listen up, everyone. This has been a very special year. My first full year teaching. I've been so happy to be your teacher, and I hope you come back to visit me next year and say hello when you're all grown-up third graders."

"I will!" Tyler's voice rang out above the others who echoed his sentiment.

"Alright, let's go," Josie said, leading them outside. She waited as each one left, saddened that the year had come to a close.

When she returned to her room, she found Thresia there waiting for her.

"I already said my goodbyes to Claire." Her face turned from stoic to sentimental and she reached out for Josie, enveloping her in an emotional embrace.

When they parted Thresia took hold of her hands, squeezing them together.

"I'm going to miss you." Josie said, feeling the tears form in her eyes. "It won't be the same without you."

"You'll be just fine," Her words were a command. "I wish I was 10 years younger so I could stay and watch you bloom, Josie. Because let me tell you. You're only going to get better. You're already a wonderful teacher, and I'm so proud I got this year to teach alongside you."

"I'm the one who's proud. You've taught me so much, Thresia."

Thresia let go of her hands and smiled. "You know what I'm going to miss the most though?"

Josie cocked an eyebrow.

"All those hairstyles. I never could figure out how to tame my own curls. It's why I've had short hair most of my life."

Josie laughed. "Mine? I never know what to do with it."

"You'd never know it." Thresia said. "It's beautiful."

"Thank you."

Thresia looked towards the doorway, then met Josie's gaze once more. "You're one of the good ones. Don't let anybody tell you different. And they will. You'll get parents who don't like something you said or how you reacted to their child, but I've seen you with these kids, and you've got their best interests at heart. You trust your instincts, Josie, and you'll never go wrong."

Josie nodded. "Don't be a stranger," she said.

"Never," Thresia said before disappearing from the room.

Josie straightened the desks and gathered up her things. She looked out over the room where she'd spent so many hours over the past year. She'd been there to comfort Parker when he'd skinned his knee after he'd raced into the room, tripping on his shoelaces. She'd sat with Jayden during recess for a whole week until she finally read her first chapter book. She'd laughed with them, been stern with them, and enabled them to strive for their best. And now, she was moving them on to the next place. While teaching in and of itself was a difficult thing to do, it wasn't the academic part that made it hard. It was rolling your sleeves up and digging in. It was holding a child's hand and leading him down the right path. It was so much more than Josie ever imagined it would be.

She thought of next year when there'd be a whole new crop of students clamoring into the room, each with their own needs and discoveries to be made. Thresia had taught at Montpier for many years, long before the other elementary schools in the city had even been built. How many lives had she touched since then? She was suddenly aware of how hard it must be for Thresia to say goodbye to it. Even with endless lesson plans to organize, parent emails to respond to and all the other administrative busywork that took up much of her time, Josie found she loved this job.

She flipped off the light and walked to her car, then looked back over her shoulder at the large brick building. A few parents walked out with their kids, and she saw Mr. Tuttle, a first-grade teacher, carrying a plant out to his car. He waved when he saw her, balancing the large pot in his other hand. She smiled and waved back.

8.

"Nice shoes," Josie said as she sidled up the driveway to Payton, waiting on the porch steps.

"Thanks," he replied, putting his feet up in the air and admiring each side.

"Are you ready to break them in?"

"Oh, yeah," he said, jumping up from the step.

"You haven't snuck in a run since we got them?" Josie asked, eyeing him suspiciously.

"I went on a walk with the Griers yesterday, but this will be the first run in them," he said. "Promise."

Josie laughed. "It's okay if you did. I wouldn't have been able to wait long to try them out."

"No, I didn't really have time, actually."

"Yeah?"

"Ira came by the Griers' the other day after we got back."

"Oh," Josie said. She tried to hid the disappointment in her voice, and found herself wondering how Ira had even known were to find Payton.

"I know you don't really like him…"

Josie didn't say anything. Not because she didn't want to, but because she didn't know how to say what it was she wanted to say.

"C'mon," she said, starting to walk down the driveway. "You can tell me about Ira after our run."

He looked doubtful, but followed her to the sidewalk.

"Three miles, today?" she asked. Payton nodded, and they took off.

While Payton fell into his groove early in the run, Josie ran like her legs weren't connected to her feet. She never quite felt her muscles relax, and almost tripped herself up several times as they wound their way through the Griers' neighborhood. By the time they returned, she was heaving and breathless.

"Not bad," she said to Payton as she tried to catch her breath.

The heat of the day was harsh, and they both looked like they had just jumped into a swimming pool with their clothes on. It was odd for everything to be so dry at the beginning of the summer, and it made Josie worry about what the rest of the summer would be like.

Once they were back in the Griers' yard, she dropped to the ground and lay back in the grass, closing her eyes. When she opened them again, Payton was bent low to the ground, his face upside down above her.

"I wouldn't say that was your best run," he said.

"Ah, get outta here," Josie said, waving him away. "Everyone's allowed to have a bad day every now and then."

"Maybe it's your shoes," he said as he flopped down beside her. "Should have gotten those electric blue ones I picked out."

"No way," she said. "These are my lucky pair."

"They look about a thousand years old."

"That's why they're so good."

"Are we going to stretch out? Cool down?" Payton asked, putting his hands behind his head, relaxing.

"We should," she said, but didn't get up. She watched as the billowy clouds slowly moved across the sky, changing their shape and size as they went. After that awful run, Josie didn't feel like moving. "This is relaxing," she said. She turned to look at Payton, who was looking up to the sky as well. "So, tell me. How is Ira?"

Payton sat up, wiping some stray grass clippings off his arm. "He's good. You know, he's different without all his friends with him. He wanted to know how I liked living with the Griers. He said if I ever need a place to stay, I'm always welcome there."

"Why would you need a place to stay?" Josie asked, suddenly feeling uneasy.

"You know, if they would switch me to a new foster home I didn't like or, I don't know, he was just offering."

"And, you think that would be a good idea?" She tried not to sound like she had an opinion one way or the other, but she guessed that she had failed just as miserably at that as she had at their run today. Payton looked hurt.

"I don't know," he said. "He's just being a good friend."

Josie winced. Ira didn't seem like the type of guy who would be a good friend, and the fact that he'd come to see where Payton lived made her feel like she should warn the Griers. Maybe she was reading too much into the cool-guy persona she had seen at the bowling alley, but the kid rubbed her the wrong way.

"Are you sure he's the type of person that you want in your life right now?"

Payton frowned. "You don't even know him."

"True," she agreed. She didn't know him, but his first impression hadn't won her over at all. "It's just..." she paused, debating whether to go on. "Well, you've made a few new friends at school, right?"

"Yeah, but Ira knows me," he said. The way he enunciated knows—like Ira was the only one who knew Payton—had Josie's next words flying out of her mouth before she could stop them.

"He just seems like trouble to me."

"Well, he's *my* friend." Payton pushed himself off the grass, standing in front of her on the sidewalk. "You don't have to hang out with him."

Josie winced. "That's fine. I just think you should be careful," she said, sitting up on her elbows.

"Be careful?" His eyes were frantic as he clenched his hands into tiny balls. The run they'd just finished seemed a distant memory. "It's Ira. I've known him for as long as I can remember. Sure, he's not the most polite guy, but he's my friend and he's going to stay my friend."

Josie didn't respond. What was she doing anyway? She couldn't tell Payton who to be friends with. Why did she care so much about it? Further, why was she letting it bother her at all?

"He just seems like a bad egg to me." Damn. She just couldn't keep her mouth shut. She crossed her arms in front of her, wishing that she could just let it go.

"Whatever. You're not my mom, Josie. I don't need your permission, you know. I'm fine on my own, and I've been fine on my own for the past year."

"And how many times has Ira called or visited you since you left? He was so worried about his friend that he didn't even try to find out what happened to you?"

As soon as she said it, she wished she could take it back. The look on Payton's face told her she'd gone too far.

"Maybe he tried. It probably wasn't that easy to find me."

Josie tried to remain calm, choosing her next words carefully. "Can you really say that Ira is someone who cares for your well-being?"

He didn't answer.

"I've never wanted to replace your mother. That's not what this is about. It's about me helping you find your way. It's about being your friend. I've grown to care a lot about you. It's not fair to push me away because of it, but I understand why you'd want to. I really do. I've been where you are, Payton, and I was lucky to have someone be there for me. It was part of why I wanted to meet you, when Katherine explained your situation to me."

Payton shook his head back and forth, a look of disdain on his face.

"You think you're like me? That whatever happened to you was like what happened to me?" He hurled the words at her. "You don't know anything about me! You think whatever she told you about me makes you an expert on my life?"

"No, it doesn't. I know it doesn't. But I'd like to think that you've shown me a little bit of who you are these past few months. And I know that you're scared, but I also think that you want more than anything to know that you matter. To know that it wasn't something in you that made her leave."

Payton frowned. "You don't know anything." He was defiant, staring her down.

Josie sighed. "Payton, my mom left me too."

She saw his face fall, but he recovered quickly, frowning again and wiping the sweat from his brow.

"So you think that just because your mom left you that you're going to be some kind of savior to me? Helping the poor abandoned kid who's just like you, is that it?"

"No, of course not...I just..."

"You just what? You just want to take me to dinner and then pat yourself on the back? You want me to enter this race and then, once it's done, move on to the next thing that will make you feel better about yourself?"

"No, I..."

"Well, forget it! I don't need to wait around for another person to drop me. I'm outta here."

He turned and started walking away, toward the Griers' house. They were only a few yards away from it, but Josie moved to follow him anyway. When he heard her behind him he whipped around, more brazen now.

"Don't bother following me. I'm done."

His cool stare came down on her before he spoke again, barely giving her time to ready herself for his next words.

"And I'm not coming back."

Josie held back until Payton had made his way inside. His words had frozen her in place, and she'd stood there, watching him go with tears in her eyes. It was as if the few seconds it had taken him to walk to the house had turned to slow motion and she was back on her front lawn watching her mother drive off, the warmth of her breath still lingering on her neck. Finally, she'd pulled herself together and knocked quietly on the door. Mrs. Grier answered and she explained that Payton had left upset, then assured her that she'd call later to check on him. She made her way back down the driveway to her car and pulled out her phone. She found her dad's name and hit the call button, turning on the car and letting it sit idle.

"Josie?"

"Hi, Dad." She smiled at the sound of his voice.

"Just putzing around the house. How are you?"

"Oh, I'm fine. What's going on?"

His voice went from distracted to alert in an instant. No matter how much she tried to hide it, he always knew when she was upset. "Everything okay?"

"Things are fine. I'm just leaving the Griers'. Payton and I had a training run today."

"Yeah? How's the little guy keeping up?"

"He's running great. I thought it'd take him a while to build up some stamina...," Josie stopped, looking out the windshield, down the narrow street, distracted. "Dad, do you think I'm doing this with Payton," she put her head down, fiddling with a thread in her running shorts. "I mean, do you think I'm doing this more for me than for him?"

"Well, Jo," he said. "I think that anything we do in life, we do partly for ourselves, but that's not a bad thing. You wanted to help him, and you are."

"But, is it selfish to think that what I'm doing even matters?"

"Did you two get into an argument or something?"

Josie closed her eyes, picturing Payton's face contorted in anger. "He just said some things that made me wonder if I'm doing anything to help him."

"Listen, Jo, there are bound to be rough patches. You've both been through a lot."

He had a point. "Yeah, I suppose," she said.

"You've got to remember that no matter what he says right now, his world's shifting. He's got someone on his side, and he's probably testing you a bit. How long has it been since anyone cared what he was doing?"

"A long time," she replied, her words coming out in a soft whisper.

"Think about this, Jo. After you argued, you guys went your separate ways, right? And what was the first thing you did?"

"I called you."

"That's right. And who did Payton call? A friend from school, maybe? I doubt it. The call you just made to me, well, it was for comfort and advice. The kind of call you'd make to a parent to mull over things and decide what to do next, and how to do it. There's nobody for him to call, Jo."

"You're right," Josie said, finally. "You're always right."

He laughed at that.

"And don't you forget it," he said, probably only half-joking. "Give him some time to cool down. But not too long. Even if he's not ready to admit it to himself, he's waiting to hear from you."

"Thanks Dad," Josie said, already feeling better, which of course made her think of Payton. "Love you."

"Love you, too."

When she hung up, she glanced up, taking one more look at the Griers' house before heading back to her apartment.

"Josie?"

It was Mrs. Grier, her voice loud in Josie's ear, causing her to move the phone further away. She sounded out of breath.

"Yes? Is everything okay?"

"No, it's not. I'm calling because I'm hoping Payton is there with you."

"But, I just left your house a few hours ago..."

"I know, and he was in his room for a long time, but now we can't find him."

Dammit, Payton, Josie thought to herself. Where are you? Her mind went to all the places she knew he could be. "Maybe he went for a run to let off some steam?" she suggested.

"We thought of that, but his running shoes are still here, and since you guys had already been out, I don't think he would have gone again," Mrs. Grier said, her voice growing more worried by the second.

Josie was already grabbing her keys when she answered. "I'll be right there."

It was an hour later when a knock on the door filled the Griers' home. Josie had been sitting at the dining room table with Mrs. Grier, while Mr. Grier drove through the neighborhood looking for any sign of Payton. They were waiting to alert the police, figuring that would create even more problems because of his foster status. But now a policeman stood before them, hat in hand, wearing a solemn expression that made Josie's heart skip a beat.

"Mrs. Grier?" the officer asked from behind the screen door.

"Yes, that's me," she said, crossing her arms in front of her. For such a little lady, she had a tough-girl presence that Josie envied at the moment.

"Officer Fredericks. We've picked up a boy—Payton Runnells. Found him at the bowling alley after we got a complaint of some kids fighting. Are you his mother?"

She shook her head. "I'm his foster parent." She looked around Fredericks towards the car. "Is he hurt?" she asked.

"No, he's in the car right there. He wasn't one of the kids fighting. They all took off. Actually, one of them crashed his car a few blocks away."

Josie peered around Fredericks, alarmed, spotting Payton in the back of the cop car. "Do you know who it was?" she asked. "Who crashed, I mean?"

He pursed his lips. "Don't have an ID yet, but from what Payton here has told us, we're guessing the victim is Ira Smalley. He left the bowling alley a short time before we arrived on scene. Payton told us he was driving pretty erratically, and his description of Ira's car matches the one at the scene…"

"Will he be able to come in?" Mrs. Grier asked.

The officer nodded. "He's not in any trouble with us, Ma'am. We took his statement about what happened at the bowling alley. My guess is he'll be getting a stern talking to from you all, which he should. He's a bit young to be off by himself. From the sounds of it, he was with this Ira right before the accident happened. The boy didn't make it. He's pretty distraught over the whole thing."

They followed Fredericks out to the driveway, watching silently as he opened the door, letting Payton step out.

"Thank you, Officer," Mrs. Grier said, putting a hand on Payton's shoulder to lead him to the house. They walked past Josie but Payton kept his eyes on the ground. She followed them up the porch steps, then turned to see Fredericks, watching as they re-entered the house. He gave her a sympathetic wave, then climbed back into the car. Josie made her way back into the Griers' house as Mrs. Grier dialed her husband to let him know Payton was back.

Payton was sitting on the couch and Josie went over to him. She knelt down, putting a hand over his as she looked into his deep, blue eyes.

"I'm so sorry."

It was the only thing left to say.

Ira's funeral service was on a Wednesday morning. It was a dreary day, the weather fit the occasion, and they'd even heard some thunder rolling as they'd entered. Josie had dressed in gray slacks and a black chiffon top, and she wore her hair in a low bun, hiding any sign of her wild curls. The Griers had bought Payton new slacks and a crisp white button-down. The shirt was a tad big, and Josie guessed that Mrs. Grier had guessed on sizing, buying it herself and leaving Payton to his grief.

They carried the closed casket down the center aisle. It was eerie, knowing that someone so young, someone she'd just met, was in there. When it passed by, she felt Payton's weight shift and his back stiffened.

Josie wasn't sure how to feel now, among the people here paying their respects. And though she didn't want to admit it, she felt a bit like a fraud.

The minister stood and began speaking. She heard crying towards the front of the church, but there was no wailing. No outbursts from a desperate parent asking "Why?" or comforting remarks about Ira being in a better place. It became obvious that Ira's demise was a surprise to no one there. Josie had gathered as much from the soft whispers of the women and veiled shrugs of the men.

When it was over, she and Payton remained in their seats for a long time.

"It doesn't seem real," he said. "I was just with him. I'd just talked to him. It doesn't seem fair that now he's not here."

Josie remembered something her father had said to her a few weeks after her mother had left. "Sometimes we have to say goodbye to people," she said, looking to the front of the church, and then returning her gaze to Payton. "And, sometimes they say goodbye to us. We're not always ready for it, but it happens just the same."

"But, why?" Payton asked, his eyes rimmed with red. He had slicked his hair over for the occasion, making it look much darker than normal. Josie thought it made him look older, too. Or maybe it was their current circumstance that was to blame for that. She reflected on his question. If Ira were alive, would Payton still be taking off to see him, his loyalty to his friend stronger than his ability to step back and realize the friendship was destructive?

There was no way to know. And although it was wrong of her, Josie couldn't help but think that maybe the events of the last week had played out the way they were supposed to, happening the only way that would enable Payton to say goodbye to his long-time friend.

How would things have been different if Payton hadn't stayed behind? Would he have ended up like Ira?

"I wish I knew," she said, finally. It was the truth.

Payton moved next to her, standing up from the pew and walking to the back of the church. Josie followed, shuffling past an older couple to catch up with him.

The lack of people in the building with them was telling. Ira had dropped out of school, so there were hardly any other kids his age in the church. Only one of the boys that had been with him at the bowling alley had shown, and he had slipped out of the service before it was over.

"I knew it was a bad idea," Payton said after they had gotten into the car again. He loosened the dark blue tie around his neck and unbuttoned the top button of his oxford shirt.

"Why did you go with him?"

Payton brought his eyes up to meet Josie's, and she wondered how much sadness there must be behind them.

"I wanted him to be how I remembered," he said softly.

"How was he?"

"Like a brother. He yelled at the other kids when they made fun of me. He'd help me fix up my bike and ride around the neighborhood with me until his friends showed up. He was cool."

Josie turned in her seat, putting a leg up and under her, facing him more. "He wasn't like that anymore, though." It was more a question than a statement. Josie didn't know, she had just assumed things about Ira.

"Payton sighed. "No. He wasn't."

"What happened that night?"

"Ira was upset. He was glad I called him, but he'd gotten into a big fight with his mother earlier in the day."

Josie remembered seeing her at the funeral. She hadn't cried the entire time, and she had paused as she exited, looking at Payton for a long time before finally moving on past the other rows to the back of the church.

"Anyway, when he showed up, he was raging. He went on and on about leaving town and how I should come with. What did I have here, anyway?" Payton paused, stealing a look at Josie. "I told him we should just head over to the bowling alley and let off some steam, and we hung there for a bit, but then Ira saw some kid from his school who'd been giving him a hard time. I knew he was going to go after him. They were hollerin' at each other for a long time when the manager finally kicked them out and said he was callin' the cops."

"That's why the police brought you home?"

"Yeah," he said. "Ira got in his car and waited for me. I just stood there. He finally must've realized I wasn't coming and tore out of the parking lot after that kid."

Josie knew the rest. Ira had run a stop sign, just missing a car going through the intersection a few blocks away. He'd lost control after that and hit a light pole, killing him instantly.

"It could've been me in that box today," Payton said, watching the last stragglers leave the church.

"Yes," Josie whispered. She reached over and swept a stray hair off his forehead. "But it wasn't."

"I wish I could have helped him."

Josie sighed. "I wish he would have let you."

"Back to the Griers'?" Josie asked, once they'd left the church parking lot.

"Can we just drive for a bit?" Payton asked. He stared out the window, watching the parking lot empty.

"Sure."

They drove south, heading out of town. Josie remembered a spot she'd found when searching out new running routes. There was a small pond, with a walking trail around it, but what she'd loved most were the majestic trees surrounding it, including several weeping willows. The place had spoken to her at the time, and she'd gone back many times since to sit by the water. She liked that it cleared her mind, the ornamental trees' branches soothed her soul, while the openness of the place, with no one else around for miles, enveloped her into a world all her own.

"Where are we?" Payton asked, once she'd pulled off and parked alongside one of the willows.

"It's just a spot I like to come to," she said.

The sun was nowhere to be seen, so there was no need to sit under one of the large trees. They headed down near the water, the wind picking up around them.

"Probably won't be able to stay out here long," Josie said, moving her eyes to the sky. "It even smells like it's going to rain."

Payton brushed past her and flopped down by the edge of the lake. He picked up a rock and flung it out over the water. It skipped twice.

"Do you want to talk about anything?" Josie pressed, hanging back.

He shook his head, watching the water where his rock had sunk, then picked up another and tossed that one in. Josie knew he must be hurting, but she let the silence fill the space between them. She studied the outline of him, then noticing something shiny on the ground nearby, moved to see what it was.

The piece of metal was partially hidden in the tall grasses between the pond and the shore. She reached down to pick it up, rolling it between her fingers as she inspected it. "What is it?" Payton asked, interested.

"It's a container of some sort." She felt a tiny bump and tried to pry it open with her fingernail. It popped open without much effort. "Payton, check this out."

He got up and moved toward Josie, watching as she pulled out a tiny piece of paper. Unfolding it, she held it down for Payton to see. "Names and dates," she said as she read over the inscriptions.

"You found a geocache," Payton said.

"A what?"

"You've never heard of geocaching?" He shook his head as if she might be the only person in the world who hadn't heard of it. "It's kind of like treasure hunting. Some of the caches have little trinkets or toys inside and you have to replace one if you take one. Those names are people's geocache identities. You can write on it here," he pointed to the bottom of the piece of paper she was holding. "Or you can sign in online and mark it to let people know you found it."

"So somebody put this here, and now there's a bunch of other people out trying to find it?"

"Yep. There are thousands of caches all around the world."

Amazing, Josie thought. A whole world she never even knew existed. She liked the idea of it, although it was obvious now that other people were as familiar with this spot as she was. Not so secluded after all.

"Better put it back then. I don't want any...what did you call it?"

"Geocaching."

"Yeah, don't want any geocachers coming after me wondering what happened to their container."

"Aw, I'm sure they have to replace them all the time," Payton said, sitting down again.

THE BLUE JAY

"So, how do you know about this geocaching?" Josie put the container back, and sat down next to him, folding her legs beneath her, crisscross style.

He didn't answer right away, instead brushing his hand across the grass between them, feeling it on the palm of his hand.

"My mom and I would do it sometimes. She said we were pirates and we had to find all the buried treasure we could."

"That sounds fun."

"It was."

"She seems like she'd be a fun mom," Josie offered.

"We did everything together," he answered. He was watching his fingers graze over the tops of the blades.

"You must miss her a lot."

"I thought things were great," he said, turning to Josie. "I didn't see it coming."

He was staring out at the water. When he spoke again his question hit Josie like a fist in the gut.

"What did I do?" he asked.

"You didn't do anything. It was her choice to leave, and it was her choice not to come back."

Before Josie knew what was happening, Payton was on his feet and moving for the car. Startled, she turned to see him cross through the field and called out to him. "Payton, where are you going?"

He turned, momentarily, to look back at her. "I'm ready. Let's go back to the Griers'."

"Why? Did I say something wrong?"

He swung his body around to face her then. "I must have done something," he yelled.

Josie, perplexed, stood up, putting her hands on her hips. "Why would you think that?"

"Because she was there!"

"What do you mean?"

"My mom," he said as tears began to fall from his face. He didn't wipe them away. All of the emotion that had been bottled up 'til now poured out of him. "My mom," he said again. "She came to pick me up that day." He paused, his chest heaving. "She came and...she kept driving. She didn't stop."

"Oh Payton," Josie gasped, raising her hands up, covering her mouth. For a moment she was frozen in place, picturing him after school, eagerly waiting for his mother. Seeing her and waving or smiling, ready to jump into the car and tell her about his day. Watching as she passed him, wondering what was happening.

Josie ran to him and pulled him into her arms, hugging him hard.

"It's not your fault," she said, repeating it over and over. Slowly, his crying subsided, but Josie didn't let go and he didn't move away from her.

"She didn't stop," he cried into her shoulder. "Why didn't she stop?"

9.

"WE'VE GOT FIVE," JOSIE SAID TO THE BOY BEHIND THE counter. He barely looked older than Payton, and she wondered if he was even old enough to be working here. He had freckles across his entire face, which could have lent to his youthful look.

It had been a week since Ira's funeral—since Payton had told her about the day his mother had left. He seemed to be doing alright, but she knew she needed to get him out. Mrs. Grier had called her, worried that he was moping around the house—or wallowing, as she had so eloquently put it during their phone conversation. Josie, unsure if it was Payton who needed to get out of the house, or Mrs. Grier who needed him out, told her not to worry, and she'd organized a day out.

"That'll be $35," the boy said.

"We can pay our own way, Josie," Sway interjected.

"No, no. I'm happy to." She handed the money to the boy, who then counted out her change and handed her clubs and golf balls of different colors.

"So, Payton, have you ever played before?" Ben asked, walking past them all to lead the way to the first hole.

"Nope," Payton replied. "Josie will probably kick my butt in this, too."

"She's pretty competitive?" Sway asked.

Payton nodded. "She was at bowling, anyway. I'm guessing she would be with running too, but she doesn't want me to quit."

"Oh, I'm not that bad," Josie said, taking out the score card and writing down their names.

"Maybe I should be in charge of that so there's no cheating," Robbie said, reaching for the card.

She swiped it away from him. "I promise I'll be fair."

"Alright, who's up first?" Ben asked.

"I put the names down alphabetically, so you are." Josie tossed a ball to Ben, then handed him one of the putters.

"Of course you did," Ben said, dropping his ball onto the green.

"The ball has to go under that big ape statue," Sway said, pointing to the hole's location. The mini golf course was jungle-themed, surrounding them in small waterfalls, wild 'animals' and exotic plants.

"What happens if you get a hole-in-one?" Ben asked.

"A little confident, aren't we?" Josie asked, watching him ready his putter.

Ben smiled. "Scared?"

"You guys do realize this is just mini golf, right?" Robbie asked.

"Yeah, it's not like the PGA Tour," Sway added.

They made it through three holes before Ben scored a hole-in-one. Payton's eyes went wide with shock and admiration.

"How did you do that?" he asked, truly amazed.

"Years of practice," he said, his voice serious.

"It's just beginner's luck," Josie said to Payton, dropping her ball next. Mini golf was proving to be more difficult than she'd thought.

By the time they got to the eighth hole, it was apparent that Josie was wrong. It was definitely not beginner's luck. Ben had scored two more holes-in-one, with Payton cheering him on more with every hole, if only for the fact that he wanted someone to beat her.

"Alright, I need a snack," Josie said, although it was apparent she was growing frustrated with the game. "Anyone need anything?"

"I'll take a hot dog," Ben said, handing Josie some money.

"What are you getting, Jo?" Sway asked.

"I think a root beer float. I saw that they had them when we came in."

"Mmm, that sounds great. I'll have one of those." She fished around in her purse, looking for her wallet. "Nachos for me, and I'll pay for her," Robbie said, handing her some bills.

"C'mon, Payton. You can help me carry stuff."

They walked to the concession stand and placed their order. "Know what you want?" Josie asked after they'd been standing there a few minutes. "My treat."

"How about one of those?" he said, pointing to the poster listing over 50 flavors of shaved ice.

"Sure," Josie said. "Which one?"

He stared at the list, thinking it over. "I'm not sure."

"What have you had before?"

"Watermelon," he said. "But I didn't like it."

"Maybe try mixing some flavors."

Finally, he looked up at Josie, overwhelmed. "You pick for me. I'm not sure."

"Okay, but I'm not sure what you like."

Payton shrugged. Josie was finding out that he really didn't like making decisions. He was opinionated about them after the fact, but if she didn't choose for him they could be standing here for hours.

"How about that one? Georgia Peach. It's strawberry and peach together. I bet that's good."

"Yeah, that's sounds like it might be good."

Once they had gathered up all their items, they saw the others had found a picnic table near their last hole. Payton passed out everyone's change, and Josie handed them each their order.

"How is it?" she asked Payton after he'd taken a bite.

"Pretty good, actually."

Relieved, she took a sip of her own drink, then stirred it together more with her spoon. When she looked up, Ben and Robbie were going over their strategies for the game, with Payton hanging on their every word. This had been a good idea to give him some male role models to hang out with. Ben and Robbie were into the game just as much as Payton was, and it was fun to see him feed off their energy, especially after all the stress from the week before. Josie really wanted to take his mind off of everything before she left for Colorado.

"You're only down by a few points," Sway said, looking at the score card.

Josie laughed. "I don't mean to be so competitive. It just takes me over."

"Don't feel bad. I used to call myself the Uno queen and threw a hissy fit any time someone came close to beating me."

"That game is complete luck, though."

"Oh, there's some strategy involved." Sway was serious, but when she looked over at Josie and noticed her arched eyebrow, she conceded. "Alright, I suppose it's mostly luck."

"See what these games do to people? They turn us into monsters!"

Sway laughed. "They really do."

"Well," Ben said, throwing his wrapper into the garbage from his seat at the picnic table. "Let's get back to the game so I can finish kicking your butts."

Josie groaned, rolling her eyes, while Payton offered an enthusiastic "At least Josie's!"

As they went along, Payton ended up coming from behind, moving Josie out of second place. He'd been getting tips from

THE BLUE JAY

Ben the entire game and the two of them were quite pleased with themselves for knocking Josie out of the running.

The last hole was ambitious for any player. It was surrounded by large foliage and had a deep curve, making it hard to determine where to aim. Ben went first and scored another hole-in-one. He then told Payton where to aim after Josie had sunk the ball in three putts. Payton lined up then hit the ball exactly where Ben had told him to, and got his first hole-in-one.

"On the final hole. What are the chances?" Robbie said, as they all cheered wildly.

"Well, Bennie," Sway said, after they had finished the game and tallied up the scores. "You won. Now, you must tell us your secret."

"Didn't I tell you guys I used to work at a mini golf course?" A mischievous smile crossed Ben's face.

"You most certainly did not," Josie said, playfully punching him in the arm. Then she turned to Payton. "And where did you come from? That was a great game."

"I had a good coach," he said, nodding in Ben's direction before picking up all the putters and carrying them to the booth. The others followed him out.

"Thanks for coming, you guys." Josie felt especially appreciative, knowing that Payton had had a good time, too.

"It was fun," Sway said, taking Robbie's hand as they exited the course.

"We'll have to do it again soon," Robbie said, before adding, "Nice job, Payton. Maybe next time you'll even beat Ben here."

Payton snuck a look at Ben, who shrugged and said, "You never know."

"See you guys later." Sway waved as they walked to their car.

Ben bent down, his hands on his knees, so he was on Payton's level. "That was a great game, bud." Then he reached into his pocket and pulled out Payton's electric blue ball.

"Don't tell on me, but every kid should have the ball they scored a hole-in-one with."

Payton's face lit up. "I won't tell," he said, softly. Then he put the ball in his pocket. Ben stood back up and winked at Josie.

"Thanks for the invite, Jo."

"Anytime," she said, smiling at the gesture. She knew how kind Ben was, but found herself continually surprised by it.

"Is he your boyfriend?" Payton asked when they were settled into their seats and driving back to the Griers'.

"No, he's a friend." Josie replied.

"But you like each other?"

"Yeah, as friends."

"Are you sure?"

Josie laughed. "Yeah, why?"

Payton itched the tip of his nose, then looked at her as if she was mad. "It's pretty obvious he likes you."

"Oh really?" Josie asked, her voice sarcastic. She changed the subject, addling on about the training he would need to do while she was in Colorado, but even as she talked, she couldn't help but wonder—if Payton had noticed it, too, it might just be true.

Josie parked in a corner of the airport parking garage, one of the last spots on that level. As she got out and opened the trunk to unload her luggage, she saw a flash of red out of the corner of her eye. She turned to look, seeing it was an older woman wearing a wide-brimmed hat in the fiery color.

"Don't worry, Kass," an older man said to her. "I'll be home before you know it."

Josie realized the woman was crying as she reached up to touch the elderly man's face, gently stroking his cheek as he spoke. Touched by the tender moment, Josie had almost slowed to a stop beside them. Embarrassed, she realized she was intruding on a very personal moment and hurried past them. Pulling her suitcase behind her, she turned back once more to see the older gentleman remove the woman's hat and kiss her gently on the forehead before putting it back in its proper place. He turned and began walking in Josie's direction. The woman was smiling as she watched him, but her face was rigid, as if it was taking all of her strength to keep that smile in place.

Josie turned her gaze away and hurried ahead, making her way through the airport to the gate. Once she was settled into her seat on the plane, she flipped open her phone and typed out her dad's name. *Abt to take off. Call u when I land.* She turned the phone to airplane mode, then slid the window shut beside her.

"Likes the window seat, but not the view," she heard a voice say beside her. Josie looked up and saw the elderly man from the parking garage.

Josie smiled. "I like the view. It's the takeoff that makes me queasy."

"Ah," he said, pushing a small bag into the overhead. "I'm in this one." He pointed to the seat next to Josie. As he slid in next to her, Josie noticed that under his green and brown tweed flat cap, he had no hair. "The name's Louis," he said, putting his hand out.

"Josie," she said, taking his hand in hers. "I couldn't help but notice you with your wife before."

Louis' eyes twinkled at the mention of his significant other. "You can't miss her with that crazy hat. She wears it everywhere, too."

"Are you going away for a while?" Josie asked, trying not to be too nosy, but wanting to be polite and make conversation.

"Longer than I'd like," he said, then pulling off his cap, he nodded and said, "Cancer treatment." Just like that. Suddenly feeling out of her element, she sat back, wondering if she should have just minded her own business instead of being swept up into his, now obviously painful, goodbye. But Louis went on. "The wife can't come this trip. Our granddaughter is giving us our very first great-grandchild, and I told her she had to stay in case that baby girl comes early. She didn't like it, but I'll be fine." His face broke out in a mischievous grin. "Besides, a man needs time to himself, ya know? To reflect on the world." He fastened his seatbelt then turned to look at her. "So, where are you off to? Denver your last stop?"

"Yes, I'm visiting a friend. Actually, she's having a baby as well, though she's not due for a while."

"There's nothing like a baby," he said, as if he were the first to ever think it. A young girl, about six, took the seat next to Louis, across from her mother who sat on the other side of the aisle. "My wife and I had five," he continued. Then he looked at Josie, considering her for a moment. "What about you? Any little ones at home?"

"Not yet," was all she said.

"I suppose you're a bit young. People wait a long time these days."

"I suppose they do," Josie agreed.

"Costs a lot nowadays to raise a child. Kass and I didn't have time to think about it. Our oldest, Donnie, well, he was a surprise. I'll tell you what, though, that boy was the best thing that ever happened to me."

Josie laughed. "Don't tell the other four that!"

"Oh, they all are—the best I mean." She could tell he meant it.

The flight attendant was going through the safety tutorial, and Josie felt around the seat for her seatbelt, buckling it and pulling it tight.

As the plane began to move, she gripped the arm rests, trying to imagine being anywhere else. The plane ride itself didn't bother her, but for some reason taking off always made her nervous.

"I used to be afraid of flying, too," Louis said, leaning to whisper it to Josie. "Now I'm an old pro. Don't worry, it does get easier."

"Thankfully, I don't fly that often," she said.

The Blue Jay

Suddenly the girl next to Louis turned and asked, "What happened to your hair?" Her mother, who had been busy digging through her purse heard her ask this and swiftly tried to quiet her daughter, "Now Sam, it's not polite to be so direct."

Louis flicked his hand, dismissively. "Oh pish, it's quite alright." He turned to the girl who was looking at him curiously. "I happen to admire directness." He took off his cap and ran a hand over his bald head. "I'm taking some medicine right now to help me get better, but even though it helps me get better, it makes me lose my hair, too."

"My medicine makes me sleepy."

Louis laughed. "What kind of medicine is that?"

"My mom gives it to me when I have a bad cough."

"Ah, yes, to help you sleep better."

The girl nodded, then looked at Josie.

"What does your medicine do?"

"Well, I don't take any at the moment," she said. "But I did have to take some medicine when I broke my arm riding my bike when I was your age. It made me pretty loopy."

"My mom says that candy makes me loopy, so I only get it on holidays," the girl said, looking at her mother, who was now flipping through a magazine. She leaned forward, cupping her hands around her mouth. "But we're going to visit my Grandma Betsy and she always sneaks me M&M's when my mom's not looking," she whispered, before opening up her bag and pulling out a large, white pad of paper and some markers.

Louis had put his cap back on and laid his head back so that it rested on the seat. Josie thought he was drifting off to sleep when she heard him ask, "So, is there a boy that will be missing you while you're gone?"

"No," Josie said, but she immediately pictured Ben's face the last time she saw him.

"Are you sure? A beautiful girl like you?"

Josie laughed. She could count on her hands all the times she'd been called beautiful, and each of them had been by her father. "I'm sure."

"Surely there's at least someone in your life waiting for you to notice him."

"Maybe I'm waiting for him to notice me?"

"No," Louis said, bewildered. "If there is, in fact, someone, he's definitely waiting for you."

"Why do you say that?"

"Because if I were 20 years younger, you'd be quite intimidating to me. Pretty, kind, smart. The whole shebang. That's a lot of pressure on a young lad."

"While I'm flattered, I'm hardly intimidating." Josie thought of Mia. If anyone fit that description, she would be it. Not her. "More like reserved and keep to myself. I don't really open up to people easily."

"Oh, pish," he said again. "If that's true, then you've got some work to do because that's not how you appear to me." He considered her for a moment, causing Josie to let out a nervous laugh. "What's his name? This boy you think's not noticing you."

"Ben," she said, before she'd even had time to think about it, and she felt her face flush immediately.

"Ben, the name of one of my grandsons. Good, strong name." Louis moved his hand to the inside of his jacket, pulling out a brown leather wallet. He opened it, taking out a small photo. "This here is me and my Kassandra. That's with a K, mind you. Yep, taken the day we got married."

Josie leaned over to look at it. A much younger-looking Louis had his arm around the woman she'd seen in the parking garage. She was dressed in a floral silk dress with a white bonnet on her head, and her hands around her stomach.

"She was two months pregnant with Donnie. We'd just found out the day before. She told me she didn't want to get married just because she was pregnant, and I said I didn't want to do that either! She'd better love me if she was going to marry me, because I sure as heck loved her. Then she laughed and said well, let's get on with it then. We didn't even tell anybody, just went to the courthouse and got married. Total strangers signed the certificate. Then, we went home to tell our parents. They were hopping mad, but we were crazy in love. Her mother cried, not being there and all. I still feel bad about that one, but when you get the right girl to say yes, you've got to act on it before she changes her mind."

"Louis, I've only just met you, but I'm sure she knew she was getting quite a catch that day, too."

"Are you flirting with me? Now, I'm a married man, but I hear this Ben fellow is available." He gave Josie a knowing look.

By the end of the flight Josie was telling Louis all about Ben, her father, even Mia and James.

"What about your mother?" he asked. "You haven't mentioned anything about her."

"My mother left when I was eight."

"I'm sorry," Louis said. "My father left my brother and me around that age, too. It's tough. Luckily, we were very close to our mother, and she did the job of two parents like a pro."

"My dad's the same," she said, amazed at the ease with which she found herself opening up to this man.

"We're lucky. My pal from grade school lost both his parents in a car accident. His aunt took him in, but she worked all the time and he didn't really have anyone. My mother invited him over for dinner almost every night, but once we hit junior high, he started getting into trouble and stopped coming, although I don't think my mother would have let him come if she'd known the crowd he was hanging out with and the trouble he was getting into."

Josie nodded in understanding, her thoughts drifting to Payton who was also on his own, like Louis' friend. Would his fate be similar? Not if she had anything to do with it.

"Louis, can I ask you something?"

"Of course," he said. "We only have a short while left before this plane lands, you know."

"I've only just met you, but somehow I feel like I already know you, or at least that I've known you for longer than this flight. Why is that?"

He smiled. "I seem to have that effect on people. And, I honestly don't know. Maybe it's my age, my illness. I don't question it. I just enjoy it. Besides, when you're 81 years old, you've only got so many more opportunities to meet people."

"I suppose you're right," Josie agreed. "Well, I'm glad I get to be one of those people. You're an interesting man, Louis. Very much so."

"Why thank you, Josie," he said, beaming.

The rest of the flight went quickly, and Josie found herself sad to see her conversation with Louis come to an end.

"Josie," he said as he watched his young flight companion follow her mother to the front of the plane. "It was a pleasure meeting you today. Give that Ben a break, will you? He'll work up the courage eventually. And if you happen to be at St. Luke's Hospital, come round for a visit. I'll be there, pouncing on the next unsuspecting person to keep me company."

"If that's true, then there are some very lucky people that will be walking through those hospital doors this week."

"You take care," Louis said, then turned and made his way up the aisle.

10.

As soon as Josie walked off of the plane into the Denver airport, she began weaving past people to get to baggage claim. It had been over a year since she and Mia had seen each other—the distance and busyness in their schedules making it difficult. She had been counting down the days until she saw her friend, and now that she had finally made it, she could barely contain her excitement.

She rode the escalator down into the sea of people, spotting Mia across the room, decked out in an adorable maternity dress, looking out the window and fanning herself with one hand.

"Mia Gregory!" Josie shouted as she rode down. Even though she'd been married for a while now, it was the first time Josie had said her new last name out loud and it sounded strange to her. Mia turned and flashed her a smile.

"Sweet Josie," she said, running towards Josie with open arms. "I can't believe you're here. I just can't believe it."

Mia embraced her, squeezing her hard and pushing Josie into her very pregnant belly.

"Are you crying, Mia?" Josie asked when Mia had finally let go of her. "Because if your hormones are going to be this crazy the whole time, I might just get back on that plane."

Mia laughed, putting an arm around Josie and leading her over to the conveyer system. "I'm just so happy you're here."

"Me too. The flight wasn't bad either, pretty short actually. I'm starving though. We going out on the town tonight?"

"Of course," Mia looked back over her shoulder. "James is waiting in the car outside. He's off this week, too, although he said he is more than happy to make himself scarce while we catch up."

"Well, tell him not to do it on my account. I should probably get to know him better than I do. I only met him a handful of times before you got married."

"Yeah, well, he's been taking the brunt of my hormones lately, so I think he's been looking forward to a break."

Josie studied her friend. She looked the same, but something was different. "You look radiant. Pregnancy really suits you."

"Oh, Jo, I'm telling you, it's like nothing I've ever experienced before. I'm so tired, but I lay in bed at night staring at the ceiling. I just can't fall asleep. My feet are three sizes bigger. Thank God it's summer and I can wear sandals. One minute I'm crying because James said 'Good Morning' wrong and the next I'm kissing him for not running for the hills. It's a wild ride, this pregnancy thing."

Mia put a hand on her belly, a look of pure elation on her face. After a minute she asked, "Do you want to feel?"

"You don't mind?"

"Of course not," Mia said, grabbing Josie's hand and placing it on her midsection. "He's been moving a lot lately."

"He?"

Mia nodded, an even bigger smile forming across her face. "We're still deciding on the name."

Something poked Josie's palm, and she moved her hand off in surprise.

"It's pretty freaky, huh?"

"It's something, alright."

Mia laughed. "I promise to keep my pregnancy talk to a minimum. Well, I promise to try at least."

"Oh no, Mia, don't do that. I'm here as your pregnancy cheerleader. I've missed out on so much already. I want you to lay it all on me." Josie spotted her bag and reached across Mia to grab it. "I'm good to go."

They walked outside to the gray sedan waiting for them. James immediately jumped out and took Josie's bag. "I've got to be quick or this one will try to lift it herself," he said, nodding to Mia.

"Maybe at one point I would have, but now I'm not so sure," Mia said to Josie, before turning to James. "I'm going to need to use the bathroom before we go."

"Go on," he said, waving her off. "But be quick. I don't know how long I can park here."

Mia turned and hightailed it back inside, and Josie made herself comfortable in the backseat while James put her luggage into the trunk. When he got back into the car, he turned to Josie, smiling.

"How was the flight?"

Josie straightened up from adjusting her seatbelt strap. "It was quick. No turbulence, either, which calmed my flying anxiety."

"Yeah, Mia mentioned that. It's so much quicker than a 12-hour drive, though."

"That's true."

"Well, this is all that Mia has talked about for the past few weeks. I think she's getting nervous now that we're only a few months away from the big day, and you gave her something else to focus on besides a bunch of delivery horror stories she's been reading on the net."

"I'm glad I could do something for her," Josie said, taking out her phone and turning it off of airplane mode. "It's been hard being so far away."

"I think she feels the same. It's been difficult for her not to have her family close by, too. My family's a poor substitute, I think. She's used to chaos, and we're a bit boring for her, I'm afraid."

Hmm, something she and James had in common. "You know that's exactly the way I felt growing up, too. But now I'm not so sure. I'd always want to go to her house where all that chatter became comforting background noise, but she'd always say we shouldn't leave my dad alone. It wasn't until later that I realized she liked the break from all that noise. It must be why she ended up with us onlies as her closest confidants."

James smiled a wry smile. "She got quite lucky finding us then, didn't she?"

Later that night, Mia and Josie stuffed themselves on enchiladas at Tres Amigos, a local Mexican restaurant. Josie, who was already full, went ahead and ordered a second white sangria before biting into another chip, smothered in the restaurant's renowned tableside guacamole.

"I forgot how much you can eat," Mia said, winking at her friend.

"Tapeworm, remember?" Josie said. She pointed to her stomach. "I think it's growing."

"Eww, gross, Jo. Don't even joke about that."

Josie shrugged. "I have to admit, I did think you'd outdo me this one time. I mean, you're pregnant—eating for two."

"I could've a few weeks ago, but now," she pointed to her stomach. "There's not much space left for anything but this baby."

Josie nodded, fascinated. She'd never really been around anyone that was pregnant. Since she'd arrived in Colorado, she'd been stealing glances at Mia's belly constantly. "It's crazy that someone is in there," she said.

"You're telling me," Mia agreed, resting her hand on top of her stomach, an expression of pure wonder sweeping across her face.

"And he's a 'he', ready to come out and scream his head off every night and make sure you don't get any sleep," Josie said, feigning worry. "That's what I hear, anyway."

Mia laughed. "You make it sound awful."

"I just want to make sure you have the most realistic idea of what it will be like. I skimmed a few baby books in the airport bookstore."

"Right," Mia said, rolling her eyes.

"Well, you can take the advice of your experienced brothers and sisters, or you can take the advice of me," Josie said. "I know who I'd pick."

"The expert skimmer for sure," Mia said. "Gosh, I've missed you, Jo. It's not the same talking on the phone."

"Yeah, and our FaceTime sessions didn't really pan out," Josie said. "That's my fault. You're the tech-savvy one. I can't even figure out how to download an app."

"Seriously?" Mia's eyes went wide, and Josie could see the PR prowess within ready to regale her with a free tutorial.

"No, not seriously. I know how to download an app."

"Thank God," Mia said, taking another bite.

"And, anyway, Ben's my tech guru now that you're gone."

Mia's eyes lit up at the mention of Ben's name. "Yes, Ben. How is our Ben?" She said 'our Ben' like he was one of the many stray kittens they'd brought home as kids, hoping to keep hidden from their parents.

Josie shrugged. "Fine, I guess."

"Fine, you guess?"

"Mia," Josie said, but Mia interrupted.

"I know, I know. He's not your boyfriend. He's a friend. La-de-da."

"So, to change the subject," Josie said, shooting Mia a look. "Are you happy?"

Mia nodded. "I am, Jo. I really am."

"Good," Josie said. "You look it. I just wanted to make sure. Sometimes with all the hormones and everything, people get confused."

"I am definitely not confused," Mia said. "Sleep-deprived, yes. Confused? No."

"And James is working out as husband material?"

"He is a top-rate husband, yes," Mia said, barely able to contain her laughter. Then, as if she had remembered something, she lifted a finger into the air, waving it back and forth. "That reminds me," she said. "Do you remember Bella Payne?"

Josie nodded, remembering the name.

"Anyway, my mom ran into her at the fitness center the other day and she called me after and was going on and on about how Bella said her mom had started seeing this new guy, but that she couldn't remember his name. All she knew about him was that he had quite a collection of bird feeders."

Mia paused, raising her eyebrows and tapping her fingers on the table.

"What are you saying, Mia?" she asked. "That my dad is dating?"

"It's possible."

"I think I would know something about it if he was."

"Are you sure? Maybe it's not that serious yet."

Josie thought about that. It was possible that he could be seeing someone. She'd been out of the house for a long time, and didn't make it back to Druid Falls as often as she used to.

"Do you really think it's him? I mean, I don't see why it couldn't be him, I guess."

"My mom is certain it's him. She's seen a car over there every so often, and she knows it's not yours. And Bella's dad passed away right around the time we graduated high school, if I remember right."

Josie was bewildered. "How do you know so much about what's happening in Druid Falls when I'm there far more often and don't know the first thing about it?"

"You've always underestimated the amount of information we Shonings are capable of uncovering."

"You mean the amount of gossip," Josie countered.

"Eh, tomato, tamato."

Josie rolled her eyes, picking at the crumbs of chips in the bottom of the basket.

"How would you feel if it were true?" Mia asked, eyeing her.

Josie shrugged. "Truthfully, I don't know. I mean, I didn't expect him to be alone forever. I'm sure he went on dates when I was younger, right? And I just didn't know about them?"

"I don't think so, Jo. He was pretty focused on you."

"So you think this is the first time he's gone out with anybody? Since my—well, since she left?"

"I don't know. It wouldn't surprise me. Can you really say that there were that many eligible bachelorettes to choose from in Druid Falls then?"

She'd never really thought about it before. "And there are now?"

"Apparently so."

"I don't remember Bella's mom," Josie didn't admit it, but she barely remembered Bella. "What was she like?"

"Oh, she was feisty. Bella was a year older than me. A quiet little thing—pretty much the opposite of her mom. I remember she went out for cheerleading her freshman year, and I was completely shocked. I mean, you have to be loud and yell out the cheers and stuff, ya know? But, she could do back flips, so she made it. Anyway, her mom was on every school committee, planned the after prom, all that kind of stuff. She's a real go-getter."

"That sounds perfect for my dad," Josie said. It was easy to sound positive when she had doubts about the origin of this gossip.

Mia shrugged. "I don't know. It's kind of weird, isn't it?"

"What's weird about it?"

"Think about it. If they get married, you and Bella will be, like, sisters, or something."

Ah, the real reason this was on Mia's mind.

"I don't think we need to jump to any conclusions. I'm sure if it was that serious, I would know about it. My dad wouldn't keep something like that from me." Josie stole a glance at her friend, who still looked worried as she nibbled at the last of her enchiladas. "But, if for some reason he's planning to run off with this...what's her name?"

"Leah."

"Okay, then. If he's planning to run off and marry Leah, and Bella Payne and I do, in fact, become sisters, well, I guess I won't need to fly out here anymore, will I?"

A smile spread across Mia's face. "Well, obviously," she said, playing along.

"And I certainly won't be bothered to call anymore, what with all my new sisterly duties."

"I wouldn't expect you to."

"I'll be so busy, you might just want to send an email when the baby comes and I'll reply when I can."

"Oh, Josie McCray, you are heartless."

Josie laughed. "And you're jealous of a sister that doesn't exist!"

Mia frowned. "Alright, I admit it. I don't want that Bella Payne stealing you away. I don't care how good she is at back flips."

"A good back flip is the key to a lasting friendship, you know."

"I can't talk to you about anything," Mia said, shaking her head.

"So what's the name of this place we're going to?" Josie asked, pushing her sunglasses up on her nose.

"Bebe Boutique." Mia flipped the turn signal on and came to a stop at the red light in front of them.

"Sounds uppity."

The Blue Jay

"It is. But, I've been dying to go, and told myself if I'm going to spend outrageous amounts of money on sweet little baby things, it would be at Bebe Boutique when I'm shopping with my BFF."

"So, I'm to blame for any crazy consumerism that goes on today?"

Mia laughed. "Someone's got to take the blame when my husband gets the credit card statement next month."

"I'll be back in Iowa by then, so I guess I'm game."

"There it is," Mia squealed, sounding like a schoolgirl who'd just seen her favorite boy band take the stage in front of her.

"What is so great about this place?" Josie asked.

"Oh, you know. They've got organic onesies, rattles encrusted with crystals. Ridiculous and over-the-top stuff that you would sneer at in your everyday life. But, Josie, this is the one time I'm allowing myself to go crazy!"

"You think this will be the only time?"

"Yeah, I can control myself, Jo," Mia said, putting the car in park.

"If you say so," Josie said, but she had her doubts.

They walked into the shop, and immediately Josie wished she was pregnant too, just so she could buy something. The clothes were beautiful, the blankets plush and the smells from the section of soaps and lotions filled her senses, relaxing her completely.

"Jo, look at this." Mia waved her over.

"What is it?"

Mia rolled her eyes. "It's a nursing cover."

Oh. Should she have known that? "Cool?"

"Jo, you've got to get into this," Mia said, grabbing her arm and leading her to another section of the large boutique. "I need you to be absolutely devoted to this experience."

Josie couldn't tell if she was being serious or sarcastic. They had that in common, their sarcastic senses of humor. It was one other thing that had bound them together in friendship, and one other reason why she felt a kindred spirit in Sway, who had in some ways become the perfect substitute for her long-distance friend.

"I am. I totally am. Look at this," Josie said, pointing to the tallest item in the place, a toy giraffe. "I think I saw this on one of those Hollywood baby gift lists."

Mia giggled. "Well, if it's good enough for a celeb's kid, it's definitely good enough for mine." She flipped over the price tag, and Josie watched as her eyes became the size of golf balls. She turned the tag to Josie.

"$500?" Josie breathed in dramatically. "Was it made by magical fairies with mystic stuffed animal sewing powers? I mean, really."

"Aw, Jo, I'm glad to see your sarcastic approach to shopping hasn't changed."

"I like shopping," Josie rebutted.

Mia shook her head. "Are you joking? This from the person who borrowed all of her prom dresses because she hated the thought of having to go shopping?"

"I just didn't want to make my dad go." It was partly true. She'd just imagined that was something girls did with their mothers.

There was a short pause as Mia realized what she'd said, but it was so short that Josie almost missed it. "Well, baby boy doesn't need a giraffe. Let's keep moving."

They browsed the boutique for a good hour, with Mia finding a handful of items to buy, not going nearly as crazy as Josie had expected, but still managing to rack up quite a bill.

"Success?" Josie asked as they walked back to the car.

"Eh." Mia shrugged. "I'm going to have to pick up a second job if I want to shop there again."

"Maybe they're hiring. Then you can get the discount."

"I couldn't work there. I'd just be asking the managers why a stuffed giraffe cost $500."

"True. So where to now?" Josie asked when they were back in the car.

Mia was rifling through her purchases, cooing at each one, glowing with mommy-to-be radiance. "Let's pick up some old movies and ice cream and head back to the house. I'm beat."

"Sounds good to me," Josie said. "But are you sure you're done with your shopping?"

"Honestly, I'm tired. My feet are swollen and I just want to kick back for a few hours. Do you mind?"

"Not at all. I mean, as long as "Some Kind of Wonderful" is on the list…"

"Of course! That and "St. Elmo's Fire.""

"You read my mind." Josie remembered watching the movies as young girls, a generation late to the party, but because Mia's older sisters loved the movies, Mia had grown up watching them over and over.

"So what kind of ice cream?" Mia asked, throwing the Bebe Boutique bag into the backseat.

"Chocolate peanut butter?" Josie offered. She felt giddy, and wished the day would never end. "Okay, I'm not picky. Chocolate anything."

Mia laughed. "I know just the place."

Once they were settled in front of the TV, devouring their ice cream in heaping spoonfuls, Josie looked up from her bowl to see Mia looking down at her belly. Her face was soft and serene and she was rubbing it gently, her billowy top moving as her hands passed over it. Josie turned away, feeling like an intruder on the tender moment.

Watching Mia as a pregnant woman was bewitching and Josie worked to understand just how her friend's life was changing. While she could see the obvious physical changes, it was the random looks and comments that showed Mia's growing love that most touched Josie. So beautiful was it to watch that she had continued to sneak peeks at Mia since she'd arrived.

"I always liked Watts' hair," Mia said, breaking Josie from her trance.

"I know. Me too." she agreed even though she never would have cut her own like that. "Can you imagine that hairstyle on me though?"

"You'd lose all your curls! Those glorious curls."

"Glorious isn't quite how I'd describe them."

"Oh, phooey. They're completely glorious."

Josie pulled on one close to her face and let it boing back up. Mia rolled her eyes, then sunk herself further into the couch.

"So what's the plan for tomorrow?"

"No plan. I figure we'll just wake up and see where the day takes us."

"I hope the day takes us to Rocky Mountain Chocolate Factory," Josie said, wrapping a blanket around her shoulders. There was always a chill in the air once the sun went down here, and she was too tired to get up and get a sweatshirt.

"That can probably be arranged."

Later that night, after Josie had changed into her pajamas, she sat on the edge of James and Mia's guest bed and pulled out her phone, searching Ben's name. When she found it she quickly typed out *Having a blast in CO. No place like it. How's tutoring?* Ben usually tutored in the summers, and this week he was watching his niece, Kiley, for a few days, and had been adamant that she and Sway understand that he was helping her prepare for kindergarten, and not just babysitting her while his sister and brother-in-law snuck in a quick getaway before Kiley's little brother was born.

Her phone buzzed. *I've heard it's awesome. I think Kiley's going to need to skip a grade by the time her parents get back.*

Jo was just about to respond when there was a quiet knock on the door. "Jo?" Mia asked as she pushed open the door. "Just wanted to say goodnight. It was a fun day, wasn't it?"

"It was, Mia."

"Do you need anything else before I go?" She asked, rubbing her temples between her thumb and middle finger. "I'm sorry, I just can't keep my eyes open."

"Don't worry about me. I've got everything I need. You go and get rested. Pretty soon you won't be able to." Josie said.

"Don't remind me," Mia said, yawning. "Hey, James has a bike ride with some friends early tomorrow, so if you hear someone up, it's probably him. Don't feel like you need to get up just because you hear someone moving around. It definitely won't be me."

Josie laughed. "You really don't have to worry about me getting up that early. This is my vacation, remember?"

"Good point. Okay, well, goodnight, Jo."

"Night."

Josie pulled down the comforter on the bed and settled in, sliding up the lock screen on her phone so she could type another message. *No doubt Kiley will b more than ready for K. Maybe she shd just skip two grades and enroll in my class!* It only took him a few seconds to respond.

:) How's Mia? Ben had never met Mia, but had heard about her plenty. In fact, for a short time he even thought she was Josie's sister.

Same as I remember. Just a bit bigger around the middle.

He didn't reply right away, and Josie had just snuggled into bed when her phone vibrated on the nightstand next to her.

Jo, how about we try out Aly & Vinnie's when you get back?

She texted back. *Sure. Night Ben.*

It wasn't until she was about to drift off to sleep that she realized that Ben's invitation was probably a date. She tried to push the notion out of her mind—surely it was just a dinner between friends. But the more she thought about it, the more she was convinced this wasn't just a causal dinner. Aly & Vinnie's was a little Italian place off of Portico that Josie had wanted to try for ages. She vaguely remembered mentioning it at school one day, but it had been in passing and she never expected that anyone would remember.

Then again, would he really have asked her on a date through a text message? Actually, yes, she thought. If he had asked in person she would have known he was asking her out on a date right off the bat, and who knows what she would have said. But a harmless text to plan to meet up when she got back? It could be just a way to catch up, and tell him about her trip. Her casual response proved that she had assumed it was nothing romantic. And he hadn't texted back after.

Josie tossed and turned most of the night, and when she woke up the next morning she was more tired than before. Mia was already up and making coffee in the kitchen. She put a K-Cup into the Keurig as Josie shuffled into the room.

"Good morning, Jo. How'd you sleep?"

"Not great, actually."

"Oh no," Mia said, turning around with a scowl on her face. "Was it the pillows? I told James that those weren't fluffy enough, but he said not everyone likes fluffy pillows. I mean, who doesn't like fluffy pillows?"

"The pillows are fine, Mia. It's just me. I couldn't shut my mind off. I tossed and turned all night."

"Why? What's up?" Mia put her coffee mug below the Keurig spout and the machine started to rumble as it worked its magic. Josie took a seat on the stool at the island.

"I sent a text to Ben yesterday," she said, ignoring the enthusiastic grin that suddenly appeared on Mia's face. "It was just to let him know how things are going here. Anyway, he mentioned going out to dinner when I got back."

"So, a date?"

"That's what kept me up all night. I'm not sure. The restaurant he suggested is really nice. Definitely somewhere you'd go if you were on a date."

The Blue Jay

"Okay…"

"But, I mean, it could just be a way to catch up, too. He could have even invited Sway for all I know."

Mia stared at her friend, whose tangled mess of curls were the epitome of crazy bed head. She reached forward to flatten a few of the strays on top of Josie's head. "Do you want it to be a date?"

Josie chewed on her bottom lip, nervously. "I don't know."

"I think you do."

"I don't!" Josie said, exasperated. "On one hand, it would be great if it were a date. You know how long it's been since I've been on one. But what if it doesn't work out? And we work together, Mia. I can't date someone casually when I work with him. So if we date, then it's serious, right? Am I ready for that right now?"

"Why not?"

"For one I only just started working…"

"You've been working for a year, and if you count the few months of long-term subbing you did before that it's even longer," Mia interrupted.

"Okay, well, there's Payton."

"Payton doesn't want you to date?"

"No, that's not what I mean…"

"He doesn't like Ben?"

"No, he likes Ben fine."

"Am I missing something then? What's Payton got to do with it?"

"You know I devote my extra time to him."

"I see. Well, I think that Payton would be happy for you to be with someone. Don't you think? Plus, didn't Ben go mini golfing with you guys? You could all hang out together."

"I guess. I would just feel bad if it started to affect our relationship in any way. He's already had to deal with so much change."

"I get what you're saying, but Jo, he's going to deal with that his whole life," Mia said, taking her friend's hands into hers. "Just like you. And me. And everybody. I mean, change is happening all the time." She smiled, pointing to her belly. "Sometimes it's good change and sometimes, like with what Payton's had to deal with, it's not so good. But who's to say you getting a man in your life would be a bad change?" Mia held her gaze, studying her friend. "Is there something else?"

"I'm just afraid," Josie said, at last.

"If you're afraid, then you've already got something to lose," Mia said. She squeezed Josie's hands tightly, giving her a supportive smile. Then, she turned to get her coffee. "Do you want some? This is decaf, but I've got others." When Josie didn't answer, Mia asked again. "Jo? Coffee?"

"Oh, sure. What kind?"

"How about hazelnut?"

"Perfect."

"Good," Mia said. "It'll just take a few minutes. Why don't you go sit on the deck and get some fresh air? You'll feel better in no time. I'll be out when I'm finished with this. "

Josie slid off her bar stool, grabbed an orange out of the serving dish in the middle of the counter, and walked outside. Mia was right, she thought as she took a seat on one of the deck chairs, setting her phone down on the table next to it. Change *was* happening all the time. She couldn't stop it. And, really, she didn't want to.

The early morning air was crisp. She closed her eyes and listened to the sounds of the tree branches swaying in the Colorado breeze, the birds flitting around the yard. Even the sounds from the cars on a nearby road were comforting in this lush landscape.

The longer she was here, the more she found herself wanting to stay. Mia had always understood her, always told her just what she needed to hear. Going home meant facing everything life was throwing at her—her dad's dating life (if there was one), a possible date with Ben, readying Payton for the race. It

THE BLUE JAY

was all so much responsibility. But here—here Josie felt a peace of mind that was going to be hard to leave behind.

After peeling her orange, she tore a piece off and sank her teeth into the ripe fruit, letting the burst of citrus flavor fall across her taste buds.

Remembering her phone, she picked it up and typed in Payton's name.

Hey there! How's the next Prefontaine? Better not be slacking just bc I'm out of town...

She pushed send. She'd sent two other messages since she'd gotten to Colorado, but Payton had yet to respond. And where was Mia? Certainly her coffee hadn't taken this long to make. Josie glanced over her shoulder through the sliding glass door, but didn't see her. Her phone buzzed.

Bn busy. Talk when u get bck.

Talk about what, she thought.

Everything ok?

A few minutes went by as she waited for him to respond, but her phone was quiet.

Josie put her phone in her sweatshirt pocket and stood up, stretching her arms. It had been a good ten minutes since she'd come out on the deck. Reaching for the door handle, she opened it and called out for her friend.

"Mia?" she said, peering around the door. "Mia, what are you doing in here? I thought you were using a K-Cup, not picking your own beans and grinding them up yourself."

She waited for Mia's infectious laugh, but heard nothing.

"Mia?"

No one was in the kitchen, and Josie's coffee mug sat on the counter, ready for her to drink. That's odd. Mia wouldn't have wanted it to get cold. She looked down the hall, then moved past the kitchen and through the living room to the bedrooms on the far side of the house.

"Mia?" Josie stuck her head in each room. No answer. Where is she? Josie knew her friend wouldn't have left without telling her. She went back to the kitchen, then walked to the front of the house. The large front door was open just enough to let in a small stream of light. Maybe Mia went out to get the paper or something. Josie pushed it the rest of the way open, stopping abruptly as her eyes came to rest on something at the end of the driveway. No, it wasn't something. It was someone. It was Mia, and she didn't look like she was moving. Instantly, Josie felt her legs push off the front stoop and down the driveway.

"Mia!" she yelled. Then, to no one in particular, "Help!"

Mia's body was facing away from her and didn't move as Josie called out her name. Crouching down, Josie felt for a pulse. There it was. It was light, but it was there. Thank God, Josie thought as she lightly tapped on Mia's cheeks, trying to wake her up.

Quickly, she dug into her sweatshirt for her phone, dialing as fast as she could.

"9-1-1. What is your emergency?" A woman's voice asked after just one ring.

"Yes, hi. I just found my friend outside. She must have fainted or something."

"She's breathing?"

"She's breathing, but I can't wake her up." she said, before quickly adding, "She's pregnant."

"Okay, can you tell me where you are?" the dispatcher asked.

"I'm not from around here. It's 409, hold on a minute," Josie said, standing up to look for the street sign. She left Mia to run past several houses to the corner, looking up into the glare of the morning sun. "The street is Rollins Road."

"Okay, stay on the line. I'm sending someone now."

It seemed ages until Josie heard the sirens. With most of the neighborhood already off to work, the street felt abandoned. A few residents began to wander out as the ambulance pulled into the driveway, but Josie barely noticed them.

"We've got a female, mid-to-late 20s. She looks to be around 30 weeks pregnant." A tall, lanky paramedic relayed the info to the other medics as they descended on the front lawn.

"What's her name?" a young, female medic asked, turning to Josie.

"Mia. Mia Gregory."

There was a flurry of activity as they moved Mia onto the gurney. Josie watched for any movement or sign that she was waking up, but her body was as still as it had been when she'd found her moments before. As soon as she had gotten off the phone with the dispatcher, she called James. It rang four times, then went to voicemail.

"James. It's Josie." She did her best to stay calm, but her breathing was erratic and her voice was shaking as she watched them load Mia into the ambulance. "I just found Mia outside the house. I think she fainted, but she's not waking up. They're taking her to St. Luke's Hospital. Call me as soon as you can."

Once at the hospital she realized she'd come with nothing but her phone in her hand. She was still dressed in her pajamas, she'd forgotten her purse and her blonde curls were probably scaring the young children that passed by her in the waiting room. She tried to call James once more, but he didn't answer and she didn't leave a second message. She had no idea what was going on with Mia. She hadn't seen a doctor since they'd arrived, and her mind was racing, thinking of what could have happened to her. Would Mia get through this? Would the baby? Josie didn't want to think about the worst-case scenario, but every time she closed her eyes, she saw her friend lying there in the yard and heard herself yelling Mia's name—her voice sounding more like that of a cornered victim running from a deranged psychopath in a horror film than her own.

"Josie!"

She turned, seeing James at the other end of the waiting room, sweat pouring down his face. He was still wearing his biking shorts and riding gloves, though he now carried his helmet in his hand.

"James," she said, breathing a sigh of relief.

"Where is she?" His eyes darted around the room. "I threw my bike in the Jeep and drove straight here when I got your message."

"I'm not sure. No one has told me anything because I'm not family." Josie put a hand on his shoulder, trying to contain her emotions. She'd attempted to get information from the emergency room liaison, a gruff, middle-aged woman with a sharp and pointed nose who clicked her tongue as she received updates on an outdated handset.

James swiftly moved toward the desk where the liaison looked up briefly, before checking her clipboard. Josie took a seat in the waiting area, watching her get up and push through the double doors to the patients-only area, returning a minute later with a doctor in tow. From where she was seated she couldn't make out what he was saying, but his expression stayed calm as he relayed information to James, who took it all in. A few minutes later, the doctor left and James returned to the waiting area where Josie sat, nervously pulling at her curls.

"Mia's doing okay," he said as his eyes started to fill with tears. "They're taking the baby out now." He paused, breathing deeply. Then he looked up, the pain etched on his face. "He's only 32 weeks, Josie."

Josie inhaled softly, covering her mouth with her hand.

"32 weeks," he said again, his voice quavering as he tried to hold it together.

"What happened, James?" she asked.

"The doctor said it was eclampsia," he paused and looked towards the doors the doctor had disappeared behind. "They think he'll be okay, but they won't know for sure until they get him out. He could possibly have lost oxygen while Mia was unconscious..." His voice trailed off and he put his head in his hands.

Josie sat back in her chair. She wanted to say something to comfort him—to comfort herself, but there was nothing to say. They could only wait.

When the doctor finally came back to take James up to the NICU, Josie had bitten all her nails down to the quick, a nervous habit from her teenage years that she'd never been able to kick. The doctor spoke to James quietly as they headed back behind the double doors. Josie thought of Mia, alone now in the operating room. While James went to be with his son, she was still in surgery, unaware of the chaos that had just taken place.

"How are you feeling?" Josie asked, tentatively moving into the room. Mia was lying on the hospital bed, staring intently at the lunch menu. She looked up when she heard Josie's voice.

"Josie! I've been waiting to see you."

"I was here all night, but took the Jeep back to your place this morning to shower."

"I'm glad. Don't want you stinking the place up," she said with a laugh, though it was a much more subdued laugh than what she normally heard from Mia.

"Have you slept?" Josie asked. She took a seat on the end of Mia's bed.

"Not a wink," Mia replied. Her face was puffy, as if she'd been crying, but at the moment she looked calm and collected. "Not quite the vacation you'd imagined, I'm sure."

"Oh, Mia, I don't care about that."

She smiled weakly. "Jo, I..." Her voice faded away, and Josie noticed her hands were shaking as she put the menu down on the bed. "If you hadn't been here..." she started, her voice quavering. "The doctors said if I had been there much longer before someone found me that..."

Josie held up her hand. "Don't say it, Mia."

"James wouldn't have been home for hours. Everyone on our street had mostly left for work. When I think about it, I can't catch my breath."

Josie reached over and grabbed Mia's hand. "You can't focus on that. You have to focus on the fact that you're safe now. The baby's safe—as safe as he can be, at least. And, you're here another day to look at my beautiful face."

"I've never seen one more beautiful," Mia agreed, ignoring the sarcasm in Josie's voice.

"Well, I have and I'm looking at it right now. I've been waiting to see it again for hours."

"How's James?" Mia asked, leaning back against her pillow, grunting from the sharp pain she felt in her stomach after the C-section.

"Easy," Josie said, letting go of Mia's hand as she leaned back. "He seems like he's keeping it together. When I got back he took the keys so I think he was taking your advice and going home for a bit."

"He hasn't slept all night. He needs some rest."

"We were both so worried. I thought your mom was going to crawl through the phone when James told her what had happened."

That made Mia laugh, but she again winced at the pain it caused her. "She's probably already checking flights."

"She is."

"I feel so useless." Mia closed her eyes for a long while, and Josie grasped onto one of her curls, twirling it in her fingers.

"How so?"

"My baby's on another floor of the hospital hooked up to a bunch of tubes, no doubt." She opened her eyes again. "I can hardly move without stabbing pain shooting through me. Everything's turned out the opposite of how I thought it would go."

"You can't plan everything. I vaguely remember someone I know saying birth plans are a waste of time because it never happens the way you think. Yes, I do remember you saying that."

"Well, you know how many times over I'm an aunt. I've seen plenty of birth plans get thrown out the window."

"Mia, you know I can't keep track of all your nieces and nephews," Josie said.

"I can barely keep track." Mia smiled, picking up the menu again, but she didn't look at it. "We're going to name him Josef."

"You don't have to do that," Josie said, feeling a mix of joy and unworthiness at Mia's declaration.

"I know," Mia said. "But, James has seen him and said the name fits him perfectly. I told him if he even looks remotely like a Josef, that's going to be his name. It was the first thing I said after they told me what had happened."

Josie was touched. She never took Mia for the sentimental type. "I'm honored," she said.

"You saved his life, Jo." Mia closed her eyes and when she opened them again they shimmered with tears as they focused on Josie. "You saved mine, too."

After Josie had left Mia's room, she wandered down to the nursery to look at the infants sleeping. Josef should be here, she thought. Instead he was fighting for his life in the NICU, along with dozens of other infants. She watched as one baby lifted his tiny arm up into the air, and as another was pulled out of the bassinet and placed in her father's arms. The man was beaming with pride, and Josie felt a pang of sadness as she realized James and Mia would not have these small moments, as they waited for their son to grow.

"Fancy seeing you here," she suddenly heard behind her. Whirling around, she was greeted by a familiar face.

"Louis!" she exclaimed, a little too exuberantly.

"Josie," he said. "What brings you here? I thought your friend wasn't due for a few months, at least a few more weeks?"

"She wasn't." Josie briefly explained the circumstances that had brought her to St. Luke's.

"Amazing," Louis said when she'd finished.

"What?" Josie asked, curious.

"What are the chances that you'd be there? It's funny sometimes the way the world works. Makes you think there's got to be a reason things turn out the way they do."

"Oh, I don't know," Josie said. She didn't know if she believed in such things. "For as many good things that happen, there are just as many bad. Things that don't work out how they should."

He shrugged, his eyes turning to the babies in the nursery. "I like to come over here before my chemo sessions. Gives me a little motivation to keep fighting."

"Is it terrible?"

"It's hell," he said, turning back to Josie. "I wouldn't wish it on my worst enemy."

"How do you cope with it? Especially having your family back home?"

"Didn't I tell you one of my son's lives out here with his wife? It's part of why I trekked all the way here to look into some other medical options. Nicholas was adamant about it."

"But you miss your wife?"

"I do miss Kass. We've always done everything together, our whole lives."

"How do you handle it all?"

Louis sighed. "I just do. I know I'm at the tail end of life. Getting closer to my ride off into the sunset. But, I'm not quite ready to move on to whatever's next. No, sir. I've still got some living to do."

Josie smiled. "I'm sure you do."

"Want to join me?" He asked, his eyes twinkling.

"At chemo? Are you sure?"

"Yeah, they'll just hook me up. I won't start feeling bad until after, and you can keep me company. The nurses will welcome the break from my jabbering."

"I'd love to." She pulled her phone out, texting James to let her know when he'd returned to the hospital. With Mia resting, she would've just found a spot somewhere in the waiting room to read or, more likely, nap. Keeping Louis company sounded infinitely more delightful than either of those options at the moment.

Once Louis was hooked up to his IV, he turned to Josie. "Kass asked me how the flight was and I told her about you."

"Oh yeah? What'd you say?"

"I said a beautiful young girl flirted with me the whole way to Colorado."

She laughed. "And what did Kass say to that declaration?"

"That I must have been hallucinating, of course."

"Sounds like a woman after my own heart."

"She's quite a girl." Josie liked thinking of the woman she'd seen wearing the bright red hat as a 'girl'. It made her feel that she and Louis were somehow invincible, which was comforting as she took in his current situation.

"How's your fella? Give him his chance, yet?"

Josie blushed, and immediately her hands went to her cheeks. "Yes, actually—though it was a bit unintentional. We're going on a date, I think, when I get back."

"You think?"

"I didn't think it was a date when I replied, but then I realized it was probably a date after."

"Did he send you an invitation? What do you mean when you replied?"

"You know, I sent him a text. On my phone."

Louis shook his head. "I must be getting too old. Is there anything less romantic than a text?"

Josie smiled, enjoying the feeling of sharing a conversation with someone that didn't involve life and death. The last 24 hours had been such a whirlwind that she'd almost forgotten what it felt like to relax.

"We're in the era of text messages and emails, Louis. The world's gone high-tech."

He snorted, his nostrils flaring a bit, making him look like a caricature of himself. "Give me a handwritten note any day."

"Oh, I would love that. But, unfortunately, that's just not likely to happen."

"A shame, if you ask me."

"Did you write letters to Kass?"

"You bet I did. She said the first one made her fall in love with me. The second made her want to marry me. And the third assured her that she was right about me."

"You did all that in three letters?"

"Apparently so."

Josie was impressed. "Like I said before, she's a lucky woman."

"Oh, pish," Louis said. "You saw Kass for yourself! She has that extra something special about her. She could have had her pick of any man, or at the very least could have snagged someone who would be able to give her a more comfortable life than I have. There were times we were scraping by. I wasn't much to look at either, to be honest." He shrugged. "But she picked me. And you know why? Because I showed her how the rest of our life could be. That I'd always love her. I'd always support her. And I'd always try to make her laugh."

"And you wrote to her."

"Yes. I wrote her letters all the time. I told you, she fell for me after the first one. You've just got to figure out your strengths and use 'em to your advantage."

"I don't think Ben's much of a writer."

"I'm sure he's good at something. Maybe he'll surprise you."

Just then, Josie's phone vibrated. It was James. *Back at the hospital*, the message read.

"Don't stick around here if you need to go," Louis said. "I've only got a little while left, and my crosswords here to do."

"I should get back to check on Mia," Josie said, gathering up her things. "This has been an unexpected few days. Thanks for surprising me today, Louis. I'm really glad I got to see you again."

"I'll be here tomorrow, too. Don't feel like you can't come say hello if you're going to be here in the hospital every day."

"I'll do that," she said. Then, surprising herself, she reached down and hugged the old man.

"Take care, Josie."

"You too, Louis."

"The boy's on his own?" Louis asked, as he and Josie made themselves comfortable.

"Yes," she said. "The foster parents he's with now seem great, so I hope it works out with them."

"He can't live with you?"

"I suppose he could if I were a foster, but no, that's not how it works. I'm the person that's there through whatever his situation is at home. Mentors help provide stability."

"I see," Louis said, taking her words in. His brow was furrowed, and Josie could see the deep lines in the skin around his eyes. In a world where youth was prized over everything else, Josie had always been more interested in older faces, wondering how they had come to look the way they did. Faces could tell you a lot about a person.

"He wasn't thrilled about the relationship at first."

"No, I don't suppose he would be."

"But we've come a long way already."

"What made you choose a boy?" Louis asked, pulling the handle on his recliner and leaning back to relax as the chemo drip moved from the IV into his body.

"It wasn't on purpose. I don't know if the other kids I could have chosen from were girls or boys. When Katherine—she's the match coordinator—when she began telling me about Payton, I just felt immediately like he was the right one."

"Interesting."

"How so?"

"It's funny. The reasons we do the things we do. You know, what ultimately brings us to the choices we make."

"Are you talking about a higher power?"

"Maybe."

His vague answer perplexed Josie.

"Do you believe in God, Louis?"

"Do you?"

"I want to, but no, I don't think I do."

"I used to believe. As a boy, I mean." He closed his eyes, as if trying to remember that time. When he opened them again, Josie thought she saw tears in his eyes. He turned to her and gave her a gentle smile. "Most of my life I've wondered about it. Never been the church-going type. But as I've entered into the twilight of life, I wonder. Or maybe I just wish. It's hard to come to terms with your own mortality. I think that's why I like to know what other people believe. And why they believe it."

Josie nodded. "There are times when I think there must be more meaning to things. The fact that I was here with Mia. Is it coincidence or something more? I don't know. How many other people weren't as lucky as Mia? And why weren't they?"

"So many questions."

"And never any answers."

"Some would say that's what faith is for."

"I think I lost my faith a long time ago," Josie said, leaning back.

Louis fell silent for a long time. He looked more tired today, which wasn't all that surprising given the circumstances. "How is the baby?"

"He's alright. He's had some tough battles so far, but pulled through them all. Mia's mom gets here in a few days. Did I tell you I extended my trip?"

"No, that's great. She'll need you when she finally goes home."

"Oh, you'd be amazed at Mia. She's so strong."

Louis shook his head. "She may be, but when she leaves this hospital without a baby in her arms, she's going to need some extra love. Trust me on this one, kiddo."

Josie hadn't thought about that. A new mom expecting to bring her baby home with her now had to leave him in the hands of the doctors and nurses.

"Where's her husband today? Does he mind you leaving them to come babysit me?"

"Oh, no. He doesn't mind. Mia needs rest, to help her recover, and I don't want to intrude when they're trying to get their bearings with all that's happened. Honestly, I think they're impressed."

"Oh?"

"I'm not one to make friends easily. So they find it quite humorous that I'm visiting a man I just met on the plane ride here."

"First of all, I don't believe for a second that you have a hard time making friends. And second, they only find it funny because they haven't met me."

An older lady across from them coughed and turned the page of the book she was reading.

"It's true, Louis. I'm too reserved for my own good."

"You've been quite open with me." He was right. Josie had felt comfortable around him the moment she'd seen the love between him and Kass. "I don't think you see yourself the way that you are."

Was that her problem? She didn't know herself?

"You don't trust yourself," he said, as if reading her mind. "You've got to trust your instincts about people. You were too young when your mom left. But you choose who is in your life now, so when you let them be in it, you've got to believe they won't let you down. You've got to trust your own choices."

"You're just full of advice today," Josie said. "What's gotten into you?"

Louis looked across the room at the woman reading. She was so engrossed in her book she didn't look up to see the two of them watching her.

"Somebody's got to reap the benefits of my mistakes. My knowledge."

"Yes, thank you for bestowing it on me," Josie said.

"It was either you or the bookie over there, and she seems to be far more interested in the written word."

"Well, you're right about one thing," Josie said as she leaned back into her chair, then crossed one leg over the other. "If Mia and James met you, they would definitely understand why I keep coming back to see you. You, sir, are one in a million."

A car door slammed outside, sending Josie rushing around the kitchen to finish picking up dishes. She quickly wiped down the counters with a wet paper towel, finishing just as she heard the front door open.

"Hey Jo," Mia called from the entryway. Josie threw the paper towel into the garbage and walked out to meet her friend.

"Here, let me get that," she said as Mia leaned into James to take her jacket off. An unexpected rainstorm had moved in early that morning and had yet to dissipate. Josie took the jacket and hung it in the coat closet as James helped Mia into the living room.

"I'm moving pretty good, don't you think?" she asked. One hand was clasped down on James' elbow, while the other cradled her belly, where her incision must have been.

"Like a champ," James said, kissing the top of her head. It was the kind of sweet gesture that wasn't premeditated. The longer Josie was around them together, the more she saw what a loving relationship they had; though, neither of them packed on the PDA, they constantly let the other know they were loved, and Josie always felt a little bit like she was interrupting in those moments. Mia would have brushed it off if Josie mentioned it, making it seem like it wasn't a big deal, but Josie knew it was. Some people searched their whole lives for love like that, and no one was more deserving of it than Mia.

Mia leaned back into the couch, her body tense until she'd sunk down into it, finding that sweet spot. "I think that was enough excitement for one day," she said, putting a hand to her forehead and taking a deep breath. "Who would've thought a ride home from the hospital could take so much out of you?"

"Do you need anything?" James asked, putting his hands in his pockets as he looked at his wife.

"I am a bit thirsty. How about a big glass of water? Oh, with ice, too. Jo, do you want anything?"

"I'm fine," Josie said to James. "Don't worry about me. I know where the glasses are. Mia, he doesn't have to wait on me."

"You're still our guest," Mia rebuffed as James went to the kitchen.

"Yes, but I'm sure you'll be ordering him around enough for the both of us over the next few days."

A mischievous smile spread across Mia's face. "I suppose you're right."

"Were you able to see Josef before you left?" Josie asked.

"We were," she said. "Jo, he's so tiny. I mean, I've never seen a baby so tiny. His fingers. His nose. But, he's beautiful. The most perfect baby in the whole world."

"How could he not be?"

"Just don't tell my nieces and nephews I said that."

Josie laughed. "Doesn't every mom think their baby is the most beautiful? I don't think they would be offended if they knew."

"I guess you're right. You forget that I'm the favorite aunt, though—because I could spoil them rotten. Now I've got my own to spoil so a comment like that could knock me out of the top spot!"

"You've given them a brand new baby cousin," James said, setting a glass of water down on the coffee table in front of Mia. "I don't think you'll lose their affections."

"So, tell me about this friend of yours you've been visiting..."

"His name's Louis. He's in his eighties, so don't go thinking he's boyfriend material." Josie shot a look at Mia, who opened her eyes wide in response.

"Me? Never."

"Anyway, he's having some cancer treatments done here, and I just happened to run into him."

"I'm glad," Mia said. She reached down to pick up her water and take a sip. "I was afraid you'd be completely bored. I feel bad that your vacation has turned out this way."

"No, no, no," Josie said, shaking her finger. "You don't feel bad about anything. This trip was always about the pregnancy and being here for you."

"Still, I'm glad you had someone to talk to while James was busy with me and the baby."

"You do know I'm capable of keeping myself occupied, right? I live alone, remember? I'm completely content."

"Not too content, I hope," Mia said, yawning.

"She isn't, but you look like you are," James said. "Why don't you get in bed for a bit and relax?"

"But I only just got here, and I really do want to spend some time with Josie."

"I'll still be here," Josie said. "I extended my trip."

"You did? They let you switch your flight? Did you get a good deal?"

Josie rolled her eyes. "Don't worry about that, Mia. Everything is taken care of. I'll be here a bit longer just to help James out around the house. I know how messy you are, and now that you can't clean up after yourself, poor James would be left to do it."

"That's definitely true," Mia admitted.

James smiled. "Thank you, Josie."

"Alright," Mia conceded. James hoisted her up so she was leaning on him with most of her weight.

"Sleep tight," Josie said, watching them walk to the master bedroom.

Once James had confirmed Mia was sound asleep, she asked to borrow the car keys, and headed toward the hospital. It might be the last day she could see Louis before she flew back home, and she now probably knew the route to the hospital better than most who lived nearby. She found him drifting off to sleep in the same recliner he'd been in the first day she'd accompanied him here.

"Sleeping during treatment now, eh?" Josie said, jolting him awake.

"I wasn't sleeping. I was resting my eyes."

"Sure," Josie said, taking a seat beside him.

"I wasn't sure you were coming today. And then, I thought, maybe you'd left for home already."

"I wouldn't leave without saying goodbye."

"No," Louis said, folding his arms in front of his chest. "You wouldn't, would you?"

Josie stayed an hour that day. When she finally got up to leave, she turned and knelt in front of Louis' chair. He reached for her, cupping her face in his hands, and lightly kissed her forehead.

"Goodbye, Josie from Iowa." Then, he let go, leaned back and closed his eyes.

"The last time we said goodbye, you moved out of the state," Josie said, holding back tears. "I was devastated. I think I stood in your driveway for an hour after you'd driven away."

"I remember looking back and seeing you there. I was so afraid for you. You looked like just about the saddest girl in the world."

"I was."

"But Jo, you're figuring things out." Mia sounded so sure that Josie almost believed her. "And so am I. I admit that this isn't the scenario I had planned, but we'll get through it. And, we'll be back in Druid Falls before you know it."

Back in Druid Falls. The words were comforting. "I'll be counting down the days."

"And if we can't fly with Josef, we'll be driving with him. Don't you worry, Jo. "

"Well, when he's ready. Don't rush it. But I'll be waiting with open arms."

James checked his watch. He was holding Josie's suitcase in one hand and had opened the front door with the other. "Better get moving so we make sure you don't miss your flight," he said.

"You'll be fine." Josie reached forward and hugged her friend. Neither of them let go—they clung to each other unable to break away, saying everything they wanted to say through the embrace.

"So will you," Mia whispered into her ear. "I love you, Jo."

"And I love you."

Finally, Josie stepped away, hesitating briefly before turning to walk through the open door. Mia followed them out, waving and wiping away tears as they walked to the car. Before she went around and climbed in, she took one last look at her friend. "You're the most beautiful mother I've ever seen," she said, watching as more tears fell from Mia's eyes. "Take care of yourself. Or I'll be back to whip you into shape. That little boy will need you relaxed and ready when he gets home."

"Bye, Jo."

She watched Mia waving as they pulled out of the driveway. As soon as they were out of sight, she started to cry. Sometimes being strong for someone else was a lot of work.

James patted her on the shoulder. "We're all going to be okay, Josie," he said.

She hoped, more than anything, that he was right.

When they reached the airport, James walked in with her, carrying her bag. "Oh, you don't have to do that," she'd said when he'd gotten out of the Jeep, too. But he'd insisted.

"Josie, I haven't gotten a chance to thank you." His eyes were tearful, too, and it made Josie uncomfortable. She always hated seeing men get emotional. She thought it was just about the saddest thing in the world to see. "Mia and Josef..." his breath caught in his throat and he paused, waiting until he was able to speak again. "They're my life. They're everything." He met Josie's eyes. "You saved my life when you saved theirs."

"James, I didn't..."

"You did, Josie. You really did."

They stood there awkwardly, Josie wanting to hug him, but feeling strange about hugging someone she didn't even know all that well. Instead she patted his arm, bringing that sarcastic part of her personality back to break the ice. "Well, it was the only way to get someone to name their kid after me."

His face broke into a smile. "Someday, he'll make you proud to have him for a namesake."

Josie took hold of her suitcase, then looked up at James one last time.

"He already has."

11.

"How was your trip?" Payton asked.

Josie moved the phone to her other shoulder, balancing it beneath her chin as she unpacked the clothes from her suitcase.

"It was great," she lied, not wanting to get into the details of Mia's scare at the moment. "How's it been here?" she prompted.

"Like I said when I sent you that text, it's been busy," he replied.

"How so?" she asked.

Payton didn't respond right away. She pictured him running his hand through his hair, making it stand up on end. He always did that when he wasn't sure what to say.

"She's back," he said.

"What?" Josie asked, not sure she understood, even though she'd heard him perfectly.

"She's back," he repeated. "My mom. She came to see me at the Griers' while you were gone."

Josie dropped the clothes in her hand and felt for the bed behind her, sitting down slowly. This, she had not been expecting.

"Are you okay?" she asked.

"Yeah," he said. "Yeah, I think so."

They were both silent. Thoughts raced around in Josie's head. What did this mean? Was she back for good? If not, how long? What had Payton said to her? And, most importantly, how was he feeling about it? She wanted to ask, but couldn't form the words.

Finally, she took a deep breath and asked something else instead.

"How about a run?"

She heard him sigh in relief. "Yeah."

"Pick you up in ten?"

When she pulled into the Griers' driveway, she turned off the ignition and went up to the door. Mr. Grier saw her through the screen door and waved her in.

"Josie," he said. "How was Colorado?"

"Oh, it was fine." It wasn't really a lie. The first part of the trip had been fine, and she didn't want to get into everything with Mr. Grier. Not when all the thoughts racing around in her head were about Payton.

"You and Payton going for a run?"

"Yep." Her eyes wandered around the house from where she stood, looking for him.

"Payton tell you about his mom?"

Josie's head whipped back to look at Mr. Grier, who stood holding one arm up with the other as his index finger gingerly tapped his lips.

"Just that she was back," Josie said, before asking, "Is he okay?"

"Hasn't said a lot to us. We're just trying to be here if he wants to talk. Honestly, I think he was waiting for you." Mr. Grier gave her a little smile, then nodded toward the kitchen. "Well, I've got something on the stove. Payton was looking for his shoes a minute ago. I'm sure he'll be right down."

Josie took a seat on the bench in the foyer as Mr. Grier disappeared down the hallway, noticing for the first time that the old floral wallpaper—the last remaining update needed on the house—was gone. In its place was a blue cobalt paint that made the room pop against the hardwood floor, white sitting chairs and tan sofa. Mrs. Grier had good taste, she thought as she scanned the room.

She reached down to tighten one of her shoestrings when she heard Payton's voice.

"Josie," he said, bounding down the stairs. When he got to the bottom he looked up, smiling. "I missed you."

"Be honest," she said. "Was it really me that you missed or the drill sergeant I turn into getting you ready for this race?"

Payton laughed. "Both," he said.

It was good to see him laugh, Josie thought. Better than good. It was a relief. She hadn't realized she had been so worried until she heard that laugh and her entire body relaxed.

"Let's get on with it, then," she said.

They drove out past the Montpier city limits a few miles, neither of them saying anything even though each of them had plenty to say. She slowed when they reached the sign that read Moss Valley and turned the wheel, making her way to a parking lot further down the road, along the edge of Sully Lake. "I used to run here when I was in high school—training for cross-country. We did timed runs, hills and stuff," she said as she put the car into park.

"Hills?" Payton repeated, sounding less than enthusiastic.

"Don't worry," Josie assured him. "They're not bad. Not that bad, anyway." Josie turned off the car and slid out of her seat, popping her key off the chain and sticking it into her shoe. "You ready?" she asked.

Payton nodded.

They'd hit two miles, weaving back and forth between the trail system and the roads around the lake, before Payton slowed to a walk, his head hanging low. The breeze was mild on this hot day, and while Josie had packed a few bottles of water for the run, she'd left them back at the car. She was now kicking herself for it, as the heat was intense. Josie pulled up so she was in step with Payton and wiped her dripping brow with her arm. "What's up, bud?"

He looked up, as if he hadn't realized she was next to him, searching her face long and hard before answering. "Can I ask you something?"

"Of course. You can ask me anything. You know that."

"Did your mom ever come back?" Josie felt her breath catch in her throat. "I mean, after she left? Have you ever seen her again?"

For a minute, Josie didn't know what to say. She knew the answer, but the right answer was different from the one she told herself. Because the truth was, she saw her mother all the time—when she slept, when she was scared, when she was hurt. Only it wasn't the mother she'd had. It was the mother she wanted.

They were walking fast, their adrenaline still coming down from the exertion of their run. Josie tightened her ponytail, answering him only after she'd pulled it as tight as it would go. "No," she answered. "My mom didn't come back."

Payton thought about this, his expression strained and serious. Tiny beads of sweat streaked down his face, shimmering in the sweltering summer sun. He took hold of the bottom of his shirt and wiped them off, as new ones appeared almost instantly in their place. He stopped walking and looked at Josie.

"What do you think you would have done if she had?"

Josie stopped, too, her mind racing faster than her legs had just been. What would she have done? Was there really any way to know? What she'd do now and what she would have done a year or two after her mother had left were probably very different—or not. She'd thought about it a million times. The things she wanted to yell. The things she wanted to ask. At first she had wished for her mother to come back, and if it had happened she probably would have forgiven her immediately. She'd only been eight years old, after all. And every eight-year-old girl wants her mother. But, now? Now, she couldn't say. The woman who left didn't know her now—didn't care to know her. Who would want someone like that in their life?

"Payton, I wish I could tell you what to do," she said. "But, I can't."

Payton nodded. "I figured you'd say that." He looked past the trees that separated the trail they were standing on from the lake a few yards away. "She said she loves me."

Josie swatted away a bug that had landed on her shoe and was now making its way up her leg. "How could she not?" she asked, playfully, not really knowing how to respond to the serious tone in his voice.

Payton smiled, but his face returned to its somber state. "How do I know for sure?" he asked.

Josie sucked in her breath. "You don't," she said.

That night when Josie got home, she flipped open her computer and brought up the search bar, then began typing feverishly. It had been years since she'd checked the name. Margot McCray. She paused once she saw it onscreen. Even after all these years she still found herself afraid at what she might find. An article highlighting a new family? A police record? Josie's heart was pounding. An obituary?

Don't be silly, Josie, she thought. After all, every single one of her previous searches had turned up nothing. Why would this be any different? She hit enter and watched the results pop up. Where are you? she wondered. She clicked on images, searching through the faces on the screen.

None were her mother.

When Ben picked Josie up that night, she tried not to notice her wavering hands or the warmth of her face. Not twenty minutes earlier, she had sat nervously on the couch in her apartment, trying to decide if she should call and cancel. Since arriving home, Josie had felt lost. Not only had Mia just been the through the ringer, but now Payton seemed to need her more than ever. But Josie wasn't sure she *could* be there. And as much as she would've liked to be the capable adult with endless advice, she had no idea what to tell Payton—any guidance being completely muddled by the fact that deep down she was, in short, jealous. And she hated herself for it. This was precisely why a mentor was needed, for situations like this, and yet, she found herself wallowing in self-doubt and self-pity, still wondering why the same thing couldn't have happened to her. Hell, she didn't even know Payton's mother. She could be a total nutjob, but the look on Payton's face when he talked about her that morning made it fairly clear that she wasn't, and that stung. Everything came back to the one thing that still kept her up at night. What had she done? Why was her mother able to walk out on her without a second thought, leaving her to always wonder?

So when Ben called to remind her of their date, it had seemed like a perfect diversion when she needed it most. But was it the right distraction? Now, as Josie sat in the seat next to him, she came to the conclusion that at least she wasn't spending another night moping in her apartment.

"I like the new car," she said, running her hand along the dash.

"Yeah, it's definitely an upgrade from the last, wouldn't you say?"

"Oh, I don't know." She pulled her hand back and crossed her arms defiantly in front of her. "There's something nice about what's comfortable, don't you think?"

Ben looked over, his brow furrowed. "Not always," he said.

The sun was starting to set and Josie stole a glance at her friend as he concentrated on the road in front of him. His features seemed especially striking tonight, and she found herself, in some strange way, noticing him for the first time—the subtle way his dark hair curled at the ends or the way his glasses sat perfectly on the bridge of his nose, never moving down so he needed to push them back up. Even his expressions seemed new as they shuffled between quiet confidence and boyish charm.

"So, tell me about Colorado," he said, breaking her out of her thoughts. "You must've had a great time since you stayed on."

Josie sighed. There was so much to say, and yet, to talk about it and remember it was just so heavy. She bit down hard on her lip, remembering the panic and fear that had kept her in Colorado an extra few days. "Things didn't go quite how I thought they would." She paused, squinting out the window. She took a deep breath. "The baby came early."

Ben kept his eyes on the road in front of them, but she saw the muscles in his jaw tighten before he glanced over at her. "Are they okay?" he asked, his voice somber.

"They will be."

Ben didn't push her for more information, and she didn't elaborate. She wanted to tell him about everything that had happened, but she knew it would zap her energy completely to relive the terror of that day. And, right now, she just couldn't.

They rode the rest of the way in silence except for the quiet hum coming from the radio. It was turned down so low that Josie couldn't make out the words of the songs, but she didn't mind, thankful that any noise was there to break through the silence. The parking lot was full when they arrived, but they were able to snag a spot on the far end of the lot. The host greeted them warmly when they entered the restaurant. And, thanks to Ben's reservation, they were seated right away, passing several waiting parties in the entrance.

"So," Ben said once their waitress had taken their drink orders. "You and I are on a date."

"So we are," Josie said, letting out an uneasy laugh.

"I have to say, I wasn't sure it'd ever happen." Ben was studying her, waiting for her to say something, but she couldn't think of what to say. "What made you say yes?"

"What made you ask?"

"Well, that's easy. I've wanted to since the day we met."

Josie blushed. "But, you didn't…"

"I didn't." He looked down at his hands, then back at Josie. "I always felt like it wasn't the right time. At first you were a new teacher, getting acclimated. And, don't take this the wrong way, but you were so inside yourself, I guess I thought you might say no, even if you wanted to go."

Josie thought about this. She had been wary of getting close to people when she'd first started teaching at Montpier, but inevitably as she got to know her coworkers, they had easily become her friends. Of course she'd noticed Ben, but he was right, she probably wouldn't have agreed to go before.

"So, back to my question. What made you say yes?"

"Actually," she said. "I didn't realize right away that it was a date."

To her surprise, Ben laughed. "I don't know why I asked you through a text. It just seemed like the right moment. When you responded, I realized you probably didn't think it was a date."

"I didn't until later," Josie admitted. "The next morning I talked it over with Mia…that was right before I found her."

"You found her?"

Josie nodded. "She was making coffee and I'd gone out to wait for her on the deck. When she never came, I went in to look for her and saw the front door open. She'd gone out to get the paper."

Ben shook his head in disbelief. "That must have been awful for you."

"I still can't believe it happened, or that things turned out the way they did." Josie remembered how she'd felt when she walked into Mia's hospital room, seeing her alert for the first time since she'd found her on the lawn that morning. "They named him Josef."

Ben smiled at that. "A good, strong name."

Immediately she thought of Louis. He'd used those same words to describe Ben's name. Was it a coincidence? She was starting to think maybe there were no coincidences.

"Mia said if I hadn't been there, he wouldn't have made it. That he should be named after the person who saved his life."

"And you don't think so?" Ben asked, sensing her dismay.

She looked up. "No, it's not that." She felt the heat on her cheeks, while tears started to fill her eyes. "I've never been so scared. I'm still scared, I think. I don't feel like someone who's saved a life."

"I don't think you have to feel any certain way, Jo."

She looked up at Ben, trying her damnedest not to cry. "I thought she was dead. When I saw her from the doorway, lying there, I thought she was gone."

Ben took hold of her hands, watching her intently. "But, she's not gone, Jo."

"No, she's going to be alright."

"And Josef is going to be okay?"

"He'll be in the NICU for a long time."

"But they think he'll be fine?"

Josie nodded.

"He'll be better than fine," Ben said, trying to console her. His words were comforting, but Josie had initially come on this date to forget about the events of the past few days, not rehash them. She wanted a break from all the seriousness—from the aftermath of her 'rescue' and the news of Payton's mom returning.

She pulled her hands back. "So, what else is new? How is tutoring going?"

Ben must have been surprised by her quick subject change, but she kept her eyes on him, waiting for his response. The creases near his eyes looked deeper, and she wondered if he had slept the night before. He looked tired.

"Well, Kiley's already a great student, so that wasn't too bad. A bit hard for her to focus, though, being as they just got on summer break and all."

Josie took a sip of her wine. It was a deep red, with a taste of toasty cinnamon. The spice, a warm complement to the cherry and cranberry flavor, was one of Josie's favorites and she drank it in, feeling her cheeks flush even more from the alcohol.

"Have you seen Payton since you've been back?" he asked, raising an eyebrow in Josie's direction.

"Yes."

"And?"

Josie rested her head in her hand, suddenly feeling very tired herself. "He's fine."

"Did he keep up with his training while you were gone?"

Josie shrugged. She didn't want to talk about Payton, either. She felt awful, behaving this way. What was she doing? This was supposed to be a date, and she was acting as if everything Ben asked was a pain in the ass.

"Josie?"

"Hmmm?" she asked, distracted.

"Are you okay?"

"Of course."

"Because you don't seem okay. Did I do something?"

"No, Ben," she said, feeling, of all emotions, fury begin to build up. "Not everything is about you."

Ben's mouth dropped open at her words. "Whoa. Where did that come from?"

If she could have sunk into the floor, she would have. Instead, she took another sip of wine. "Nowhere. Nevermind."

"Listen, Josie. You don't have to tell me what's going on. If you don't want to, I respect that, but don't make me feel like shit because I cared enough to ask."

They were both quiet. "I'm sorry, Ben. I shouldn't have come. I thought it would be a distraction, but it's—it's just not."

"You went out with me as a distraction?"

"No, that's not what I meant." Josie tried to think of how to explain herself, but wasn't quick enough.

"Maybe we should go." Ben waved at the waiter, gesturing for the bill.

Josie hung her head. "Alright," she mumbled.

When they pulled in front of her apartment building, Josie turned to Ben, who hadn't spoken since they left the restaurant. "I'm sorry, Ben."

"It's not a problem. I should have realized you weren't interested."

"It's not that."

"Really?" he said, the hurt in his eyes evident. Josie turned away, ashamed because she knew she had put it there. "Because it sure feels like it."

"Payton's mom is back," she said, simply. "My best friend almost died. Her baby almost died." Josie's heart was pounding, and her voice was growing louder with each word. She used them as excuses. Excuses for treating him badly, and she hated herself for it. But what could she say now? The damage was done.

Ben's arms were crossed in front of him, but he was listening, watching her carefully.

"I'm sorry," he said.

"I'm sorry, too," she said. Then she lifted the handle and walked back to her apartment, wondering if things could get much worse.

"What were you saying?" Josie asked, glancing up from her pancakes.

"This blasted pan. Everything sticks to it." She watched her dad scrape the spatula across the bottom.

"Did you spray it?"

"I always do, but it makes no difference." He sighed, throwing the spatula onto the counter and sending a bit of the scrambled eggs he was cooking flying in the opposite direction.

Josie stood up and leaned over her dad's shoulder. "Dad, you didn't use the right pan. You need the non-stick one."

She thought she heard him grumble as he picked up the larger spatula—or as Josie had always called it—the pancake flipper.

"So," Josie said as she picked up the paper and flipped through, trying her best to seem distracted. "Before all the chaos surrounding Josef's birth, Mia might have mentioned a bit of Druid Falls gossip to me..."

"I couldn't guess what. That family knows everything about everyone in this town."

Josie had to laugh. John McCray was as much of a gossip as anyone else who lived in Druid Falls. "Well, in fact, it had to do with you, Dad."

His shoulders tensed abruptly.

"Me? What gossip could there possibly be about me?"

"You and perhaps a new lady friend?" Josie raised an eyebrow just as her dad turned around. "Dad, have you been holding out on me?"

At first his face gave nothing away. Finally, a broad smile broke out stretching from one ear to the other. "Ah, I should have known something would get around to you. Sometimes this town is just too dang small for my taste."

"So it's true?"

He crossed his arms in front of his chest. The oil the hash browns were cooking in crackled behind him, but he'd all but given up on salvaging those anyway.

"It is."

"Is it serious?"

"You're hearing about it, aren't you? You think I'd let the whole town gossip about me if it wasn't serious?" He had a twinkle in his eye that Josie hadn't seen in a long time. "What did Mia tell you?"

"That doesn't matter. I want you to tell me."

He turned around and flipped the last two pancakes, and spooned up a bite of hash browns, tasting them. "These aren't too bad. You want some?"

"Why not?" She waited for him to dish some up, then took a big bite. A little burnt, but not so bad. For some reason, she never cared how well they were cooked. Too done. Not done enough. She doused them in ketchup and pepper and they tasted like just about the best breakfast food there ever was. "I can't believe you've been holding out on me. Tell me everything."

"Well, it was a few months ago. Actually right after you and Payton were here to clean the feeders. I'd run up to the Silver Fox, just to look around. Cal—you know Cal, he taught biology at the high school..."

"Mr. Metchum."

"Cal Metchum. Thank you." He set his plate down across from Josie and drizzled some syrup over his pancakes and hash browns. "Anyway, we got to talking, and before you know it I'd spent most of the afternoon in that antique store. By the time I left, it was raining pretty steady. I got back into town and there she was. Walking down Ash in a downpour." He paused and put his fork down. "Josie, I've had my breath taken away before by a beautiful woman, but let's just say, that's not what happened. I rolled up next to her to offer her a ride home and she looked—well, if I'm being truthful—she looked a plain mess. Her hair was soaked. Makeup was running. She clearly hadn't expected the rain. I wasn't sure she'd get in with me but she looked back down the road she'd been walking and ran around to the other side of the truck. She turned towards me and said "I'm Leah Payne." I drove her home and she invited me in for some hot tea. She didn't even go dry off or fix her hair. She just put the kettle on the stove and started jabbering about some movie she'd just seen." Her dad took a bite of pancake, then licked his lips, a small drop of syrup spilling into the gray of his beard. "I fell for her right then."

"Because she didn't fix her hair?"

"More than that, Jo. Her passion as she spoke. The way she was just unaffected by however she might appear to me. She was happy to have my company, and I was happy to have hers. I think we've seen each other every day since."

"Why didn't you tell me?"

He took a sip from his coffee. "I was going to."

Josie rested her chin on her hand. "I'm happy for you, Dad."

"And what about you, Josie? Any men in your life, besides that of the school-age variety?"

"As a matter-of-fact, yes."

"Oh really?"

"This one's of the elderly variety, though."

Her father, skeptical, set his coffee mug down on the table and situated himself a little straighter in his chair. "Oh?"

"Relax, Dad," she said and preceded to tell him about Louis.

"Sounds like my kind of guy."

"You'd probably get along with him great. Unfortunately for me, he was taken quite some time ago." They were quiet a moment, and Josie fidgeted with the newspaper again. "There is someone else that I met—I met him last year, but things..."

"Yes?"

"Well, they're complicated. I mean, for me."

"And why is that?"

Why, indeed? "I'm not sure. I work with him. And we're friends, or at least we used to be..."

Her father didn't say anything. He took a bite of the half-burnt hash browns instead.

"Anyway, I've got a lot going on right now, ya know?" Who exactly was she trying to convince?

"Well," he said, finally. "I'm sure you'll figure it out."

12.

"Why did you start running?"

She and Payton were sitting on a hill near a school playground. Although it was summer, the outdoor playset was swarming with children of all ages, their parents close by watching them run from slide to swing and back again. They'd run a short distance, but the heat had been worse than Josie had anticipated, and they'd decided to walk instead, coming upon the school and stopping for a cool drink at the fountain before plopping down in the shade.

"I joined cross country in middle school. I wasn't very good, but after a while on the team, I had learned to enjoy it. And I just kept running. I think a lot of runners start out that way—and then they find they can't stop. It becomes part of who they are."

"And now you love it?"

"I wouldn't say I love it. It's hard to find motivation sometimes. I think the part that appealed to me so much then and still does now is that no one depended on me, and I didn't depend on anyone else to do it. If I failed, it was my fault. If I succeeded, it was because of my own hard work. So many other things required the acceptance of teammates and figuring out how to win together. With running I just had to run."

"But you still had to win as a team, didn't you? When you were running in school?"

"The top runners did, but like I said I was never that good at long distances. I just liked doing it."

Payton thought about this. "So you wanted to be on your own? Doing your own thing?"

Is that what she meant? "I think I was comfortable with things being that way, yes," she said, feeling, for the first time, unsettled for thinking that way.

She plucked a dandelion from the ground, wrapping her fingers around it tightly, then blew the fluff into the grassy field.

"Were you lonely?"

How do you answer a question like that? Sometimes she still was lonely.

"Are you?" Josie asked.

Payton shrugged.

"I had Mia. And my dad. I read a lot, like you, daydreaming about how my life would turn out. And I ran. Running kept me company."

She looked out across the field to the playground a few yards away. Kids ran up the slides and hung from the monkey bars, flailing their arms wildly. They laughed and chased each other—grabbed for their friends and yelled to each other from across the playground. It reminded her of when she was in school, though she would have been curled up by the side of the building with a notebook on her knees.

"I shut a lot of people out, Payton. It's not something I would do again if I could go back in time. It's painful to miss out on the experience of connecting, really connecting with people. I wouldn't want that for anyone, especially not you."

Josie stopped, realizing the words she was saying were things she had never even admitted to herself before.

"I know you're confused—and hurt. I know you probably have a million questions racing through your mind, and I hope that you get answers to them. But if you don't, don't think that one person is enough to shatter you—because no matter what there are always people out there who want to be there for you." She waited for him to look at her. "Always."

They got up to go, the voices of the children playing lingered in the air as they walked from the park, like the echo of a cheering crowd in the last seconds of a championship game. "It wouldn't be so bad," Payton said once they were on their way back to the Griers'.

Josie adjusted her hat, tucking in the stray curls that had made their way out of her ponytail. "What's that?" she asked.

"Turning out like you."

"He's asleep," Mia said, her voice full of feeling.

Josie tried to picture Josef's face, his small features as he slept. Mia had sent some photos of him by email the past few days. He was growing, but his tiny body was a reminder of the uphill battle in front of him.

"Jo, I got to hold him today."

"Finally! Was it amazing?"

"I'm not kidding when I tell you I cried the entire time."

"Happy tears?"

"Yes, of course. Maybe a few sad ones that I had to wait so damn long."

"Well, I'd say those are completely warranted."

Mia laughed. "So, what's going on there? I've been meaning to check in on how your date went."

"How it didn't go is more like it."

"You didn't go?"

"No, sorry. We went, it just didn't end well."

"Oh," Mia's voice was soft, and she waited for Josie to continue.

"I don't know, Mia. What am I doing?"

"Talking to me?"

"Yes, but what am I doing? With my life?"

"Josie, don't get all melodramatic. You're doing lots. You've just got to get your head together, ya know? You've got some work to do, but you're not a lost cause."

You've got some work to do. The same words that Louis had used. It was comforting in that moment to hear them. People were rooting for her. They wanted her to move forward, to succeed. Just like she wanted Payton to.

"Mia, you don't even know it, but you just said the exact words I needed to hear."

"Uh, what'd I say, again?" she asked.

"It doesn't matter. If you were here, though, I'd kiss you."

"Well, great. I'm glad I could help."

"You did. You really did."

"So what now?"

"I've gotta go."

"What? Why?"

"I've got some work to do," she said. "And for once, I know what I need to do."

Josie knocked on the door, pounding her fist so hard that she stopped mid-knock to massage it with her other hand. Her knuckles were red from the force.

When it finally opened, she had to stop herself from spilling out the speech she'd been going over in her head, again and again.

It wasn't him.

"Josie?"

"Uh, hi, Sway," she said, catching her breath. "Is Ben here?"

"No, I haven't seen him all day."

"Oh," she said, her disappointment evident. Of course he wasn't here.

"Do you want to come in?" Sway offered, opening the door wider.

The Blue Jay

"Oh, no, that's okay. I'm sure you're busy."

"Not too busy for the company of a friend," she said. "C'mon, Josie. I'm sure he'll be back soon. Why don't you just come in and wait?"

Josie conceded. "Alright. But only for a minute. I've got somewhere else I need to be."

Sway held the door open as she entered the house. It was older, like the Griers', but not as nice, being a rental. No updates had been made to it, making each room different from the next. There was no fluidity from room to room, but there was something about it that seemed homey. Josie couldn't quite put her finger on it, but whenever she'd been in the place it had wrapped itself around her like a familiar old sweater.

"I was just fixing a sandwich," she said, leading Josie to the kitchen. "Turkey and Swiss...interested?"

"No thanks," Josie replied. Her stomach was in knots and the thought of eating something made her queasy.

"So, Ben mentioned you were in Colorado. How was that?" Her eyes were wide with curiosity, reminding Josie that her visit with Mia had started out as a vacation.

"Yeah," she said, taking a seat at the kitchen island as Sway flitted about, removing items from cupboards to make her sandwich. "She ended up having the baby early while I was there."

"Oh my God," Sway said, suddenly whipping around. "Is she okay? Is the baby okay?"

"Yes, I mean, I think they are both going to be fine," Josie said. "She had a little boy."

"You know, I was born early, too," Sway said, turning back to the counter. "I turned out just fine. I'm sure Mia's son will, too."

"Did you spend time in the NICU?"

"Yep, not long, maybe two weeks. I was early, and had trouble breathing, according to my mom at least."

"I don't know how people do it," Josie said. "Josef will have to be in the NICU for at least a month, maybe longer."

Sway shook her head. "My mom hated it. I mean, she was grateful for the medical support from the doctors and nurses, but she said leaving me there every day was devastating. Her hormones were through the roof, and all she wanted to do was hold me. She can barely even talk about it—and I was there for a relatively short time for a NICU patient."

"Yeah, Mia amazed me. She was so calm the whole time she was in the hospital—even when she was discharged and had to leave Josef there, she didn't cry. Maybe she was just thankful he was alive. I would have been a complete wreck if it was me, but not Mia."

"I think when you become a mom you have a special suit of armor that is impenetrable. She has to stay strong because now there is someone that absolutely needs her to."

"I think you're right," Josie agreed, remembering Mia's face after she'd come back from visiting Josef. She'd looked like someone about to go into battle. "So, you're not sure when Ben will be back?"

"No," Sway said, turning to look at the clock. "I'm not sure when he's tutoring, when he's not. And, if I'm being honest, I haven't really been around much."

"Staying at Robbie's?"

Sway gave her a sheepish grin. "Yeah."

"Well, if you do see him, let him know I stopped by," Josie said as she stood up.

"You're going?"

"Sorry. I've got a meeting to get to."

"For school?"

"Not exactly." Josie started to head for the door.

"I'll let him know."

"Thanks, Sway."

"I hope everything turns out okay for your friend and the baby," she said.

"I'm sure it will." Josie waved goodbye and headed down to her car, hoping she hadn't damaged things with Ben beyond repair. At least she wasn't going to let one man in her life down. She thought of Payton the previous day, pleading with her to do him a favor, and she put her car into drive to keep her promise.

"Thanks for meeting me."

The words hung in the air between them and Josie shifted uncomfortably in her chair, not sure how to respond. She'd been delaying this particular meeting for a while, not wanting to have whatever conversation this woman wanted to have. But Payton had been adamant that she meet with her, texting her every day over the past week until she'd had to respond with more than just *We'll see*.

"Payton's told me so much about you these past few days. In fact, he wouldn't stop talking about you. It really," she paused, folding her hands together on the table, taking a deep breath. "It really means a lot to me that you're here."

She was a pretty woman—beautiful even. While Josie could hardly tame her mass of blonde curls, letting them go in whichever direction they fell unless she tied them back in a long ponytail, the woman before her looked polished, her short layers giving her an immaculately pulled-together look. When Josie had walked into the coffee shop, she'd known it was her right away, seeing that red hair, an exact replica of her son's apart from the few lighter hairs that were beginning to gray.

"Why did you want to meet with me, Ms. Runnells?" Josie asked, more sternly than she'd intended.

"It's Harris, actually," she said. "Payton's got his dad's name. We never married." The woman looked down sheepishly, rubbing her naked ring finger. "And, please, call me Nicole."

"Okay, Nicole," Josie said, her tone biting through the pleasant niceties. "Why did you want to meet with me?"

"I wanted a chance to explain myself."

Josie felt her eyebrows raise in surprise. "You don't owe me an explanation," she said.

"I do." Nicole was fidgeting with her hands, breathing quickly. It was obvious to Josie that she was incredibly nervous, but Josie, usually the first to subdue any awkwardness, wasn't letting Nicole off the hook. "What I did," her breath caught in her throat. "I'm not proud of it. What I did was horrible. It was wrong—and I know it. I don't know if Payton will accept me back into his life. I don't know anything. But, I have to try. I've just got to. And you're the person who will be able to help me most."

Josie was stunned. "Help you? Me?"

"If Payton thinks you are on board…"

"Wait," Josie interrupted. "You want me to tell Payton to forgive and forget, is that it?"

"No, no," Nicole said, flustered, her eyes darting up and down from the table to Josie in rapid succession. "Of course not. I just want to explain myself. I know he's confused. I don't want to push him into anything. I've been spending a lot more time with him, but I know he's afraid to really let me in. And I don't blame him. I just thought that maybe, if you and I got to know each other, that maybe Payton would realize it's okay to trust me again."

"I see." Underneath the table, she cracked a few fingers before balling her hands into fists, squeezing them tight. "And *should* he trust you?"

Nicole chewed on her bottom lip, her eyes burning into Josie, pleading with her.

"Do you want my honest opinion, Nicole?"

She nodded, her red hair bouncing just above her shoulders.

"You're going to have to let Payton do this in his own time. The fact that he's seen you as much as he has, well, let's just say that it's probably more than I'd be willing to see you if you were my mother."

Josie stopped and took a sip of her coffee.

The Blue Jay

"I wasn't in my right mind," Nicole said, finally. "I was two months behind on rent. I'd just been let go from my job. That day," she put her head into hands, covering her face. She rubbed at the corners of her eyes as if trying to shut out the thoughts that might be running through her head. "—it started just like any other day." She looked up, staring out the window. "Payton didn't know I'd lost my job. He didn't know anything about the situation we were in. That morning I'd packed a suitcase, thinking I'd pick him up from school and we'd leave—start an adventure, just he and I. We'd find somewhere else to go and start fresh."

"But, instead you left him there," Josie said, furious, trying to keep control of her voice. "You looked at your own son's face as you drove by and you..." she paused to compose herself. "...you kept driving."

Nicole's bottom lip trembled.

"I thought it would be for the best."

"To be in foster care?"

"To be in a house," she said, tears beginning to stream down her face. "To have a roof over his head and food to eat."

"He didn't even know why you left. He didn't know anything except that you did leave. Your explanation is that it was for the best, but he needed you."

"I know that now." Her voice was a whisper, and she dabbed lightly at her tears with a tissue. "You know I was young when I had Payton. His father, he wasn't interested in sticking around. I'd run off with him as soon as I graduated high school, and gotten pregnant a few weeks later. He stayed until Payton was a few months old. I thought we could be a family. I wanted it to work so badly."

Nicole put the tissue back in her purse, taking a deep breath before meeting Josie's eyes. "I couldn't go home—not after the way I'd left. I was too proud. We made it for a while. Quite a while, actually. But then things started to fall apart, and I couldn't handle it."

Josie didn't move. Her heart was beating so hard, she thought it was going to beat right out of her chest. How could this woman just give up her child?

Josie wanted to scream at her. She wanted to get up and walk away and tell Payton to do the same. Instead, she took a deep breath.

"What did Payton say when he saw you?" she asked.

"He didn't say anything. I couldn't tell if he was angry or happy. He just looked at me for the longest time."

Josie pictured Payton in that moment—shocked and confused. She imagined a part of him wanting to run into her arms, grab her face and press it down close to his own and never let go, while another part of him held back, smart enough not to place a lot of confidence in a woman who'd abandoned him.

"He asked if I was back for good, and I told him I was," Nicole said, Josie hanging on each of her words, as the background noise of the café melted away. Josie only heard Nicole. "Then he didn't say anything. I was so afraid. I'd pictured him yelling, screaming. I thought he'd hate me for sure."

"Me, too," Josie agreed.

"But, he didn't," she said. "He walked up to me. I put my hands out to him, and he hugged me. He accepted me."

Josie was silent. She looked out the window, spotting a bird, pecking something on the sidewalk—probably a crumb that had fallen off someone's pants as they walked back to their car. The tiny bird grabbed at it several times, not giving up, yet never getting it into its mouth. As she watched, the bird turned enough so she could see the back of it, where its blue, black and white plumage could be seen. She stared transfixed, then turned back to Nicole. "So, why do you need my help? If Payton's accepted you back, I mean?"

Nicole sighed. "It's not that simple. I think he's scared to lose you. If I come back, what will happen to you? He's afraid he has to choose, and like I said, he doesn't completely trust me."

"He's not going to lose me." She looked down at her hands, then back up at Nicole. "What made you come back?" she asked. "You were gone a long time. Over a year, right? What made you come back?"

Nicole's expression changed from one of pleading to one of sadness. She looked heartbroken, and to Josie's surprise, it pained her to see it. The anguish on her face was genuine—making it difficult for Josie to completely write it off.

"I thought of him every day. Every moment. I worked three different jobs, at first I was sleeping in my car until one of the gals I worked with cleaning hotel rooms offered to let me sleep on her couch for a few weeks. She didn't make me pay rent, so long as I helped out with the utilities and bought my own food. I worked so much I was hardly even there, anyway. Finally, she asked me why I was working so much—by then I'd saved up enough to start renting a place of my own, but she liked having me there, so I stayed." Nicole shook her head. "I couldn't answer her. At first I'd needed shelter, food, clothes, but working so much, I slowly built up a small savings. In the end I realized I'd been doing it so I could come back. I wanted to be able to redeem myself, to show Payton that I did want him. But, once I realized that, it also became obvious that what I'd done..." Nicole stopped, her arms crossing as she hugged herself tightly. "I knew he might not forgive me. I just kept working. I saved every penny, and when I thought I had enough, I came back."

"Why didn't you go home?" Josie asked. "Surely your parents would have welcomed you both, helped you get on your feet?"

Nicole shook her head. "It wasn't that kind of home."

Josie took another drink, letting Nicole's words sink in. "I'm trying to understand, Nicole. I really am."

Nicole had a long road ahead of her. She'd devastated her son when she cast him aside with no explanation. While she made it sound like she had no choice, she did. Her options were limited, but she had them, and she'd still chosen to leave—and not just leave, she'd left without her son.

But she'd come back. She was trying to make things right. After the way she'd left, and knowing Payton could hate her—which, in Josie's opinion he had every right to do—she'd come back to take her chances.

"Would you do it again?" Josie asked, the question spilling out before she'd even had time to mull it over herself. As soon as the words were out of her mouth, she wanted to take them back. Whatever Nicole's answer was, it wouldn't change anything. Payton had been hurt—deeply. Nothing would change that now.

To Josie's surprise, Nicole smiled. "I would." The words slipped out effortlessly. "If I knew things would turn out like this, I would. Somehow, I was able to find three jobs. That would have been impossible here. I worked my ass off, too, and I wouldn't have been able to do that if I'd had Payton with me. I know he had some trouble, being in foster care and all—if I could change anything it would be that, but then he met you. And Josie, I've never seen him so good. I mean, even before this happened. I can't explain it, but he was headed for trouble."

"Was he?"

"He had this friend—Ira. He was bad news, but Payton was nuts about him."

"Yes, I met him."

Nicole looked surprised. "You did?"

"Payton and I ran into him and a few of his friends a few months ago. The two of them hadn't seen each other—well, in a long time." Josie paused, wondering how she should break the news of Ira's death to Nicole. "He passed away not long after that."

Nicole lowered her head, twisting her napkin between her fingers. "I didn't know."

Josie didn't know what to say. She'd never relayed the news of someone's death before and it felt strange to do so in this setting. She didn't know Nicole, and she'd barely known Ira.

"How did he die?" she asked, finally.

— 179 —

"He was speeding and lost control of his car," she answered. Then, more because she was curious about how Nicole would react, she continued. "It happened only a few minutes after Payton got out."

Nicole's eyes went wide, and for a moment Josie thought she might start sobbing uncontrollably. She recovered quickly, wiping the shocked expression off her face as quickly as it had appeared. "You must think I'm pretty horrible," she said.

"I'm trying to keep my own opinions out of it," Josie said.

"I mean, it's bad enough I left him, right? And now you're telling me he could have died?"

"I'm telling you what happened."

Nicole took a deep breath, shutting her eyes together tight. When she opened them a few tears slid down her cheek. "Payton was always fascinated by him," she said. "He saw him as an older brother, and you know, Payton didn't have a lot of friends. He's a quiet kid, keeps to himself. He was always reading, and I think the other kids thought he was kind of lame."

Josie smiled, thinking of all the times she'd seen him with his head buried in a book over the past few months. She hadn't thought about how that would seem to his peers, only that it suited her personality so well. They'd ended many of their visits, both their heads buried in a book, sharing a laugh over some clever dialogue and enjoying the swish of the pages as they read.

"At any rate," Nicole continued. "Ira took him under his wing. At first I was glad—that Payton finally had somebody on his side, ya know? But, it wasn't long before my relief turned to worry."

Josie clamped her teeth together, keeping herself from spouting off the numerous reasons her worrying didn't mean shit. "Why else did you want to see me?" Josie asked.

Nicole didn't answer right away, her eyes darting around the shop as she decided how to respond. "I wanted to see if Payton was right about you," she said.

"What do you mean?"

"He said you were like him. That, when he met you, he knew right away that you saw him—really saw him, like you already knew him or something."

Josie considered this. She had felt it, too—kindred spirits. "And what's your impression?"

"I think he was pretty spot on," Nicole said, then tilting her head to the side, she added, "Payton's a sensitive kid—he'd give his last nickel to the bum on the corner, without a second thought. He's got emotions that are larger than life if he lets you see them, and a heart that doesn't know how not to love." Nicole waved a hand in the air like she was batting away a fly. "Look, I hardly know you, Josie, so I've no right to assume anything, but I get the feeling the reason you're so skeptical about my return is that you know better than anyone what Payton went through. And the reason you're here meeting with me, is because, like Payton, your heart is just as big."

Josie looked out the window, wondering if she was right. Had she really come here to tell Nicole off, like she'd been ready to do when she sat down? Or, had she been hoping all along that this woman she'd convinced herself to hate would change her mind? Did Nicole deserve forgiveness? A reprieve? Was it wrong for someone to do something so terrible and still expect to be redeemed? Was it silly to have hope?

As Josie's eyes fell back on the little bird outside, she watched as he finally took hold of the crumb and clamped it securely inside his beak. Then, he spread his wings and took off.

No, Josie thought. Surely, there was always hope.

With her final step, Josie let out a deep breath. Her last long run before the race. Eight miles. Not bad, she thought as she turned down the volume of her music. The parking lot was quiet. The sun was just beginning to set. Josie could feel a light breeze on her skin, and heard it shake the leaves of the trees surrounding her. One thing she loved about summer and always had—the sounds were even relaxing. She found herself lingering back, not wanting to go inside.

Her thoughts drifted to Ben. Why did she keep pushing him away? What was she so scared of? She hadn't seen him since their date, and their friendly banter through text had stopped completely. After stopping by his place and talking to Sway, it was apparent that he hadn't told her anything. So where was he? Had she royally screwed things up, as it seemed she was destined to do lately? She wanted him to be at the race, not just for her, but for Payton. Would he be there?

And he wasn't the only one she was worried wouldn't show up. While Payton had skipped out on their last two runs, he had assured her he would be at the race next Saturday. Josie knew how hard he had worked over the summer, but with Nicole back in town, he'd been increasingly torn between training and spending time with her. It was completely understandable. Josie didn't fault Payton for wanting to spend time with his mom. But she knew how hard he had worked to get ready for this run. It was important to him, and important to Josie that he reap the benefits of his hard work.

She kicked at a fallen tree limb, feeling a rogue branch brush the side of her leg. Josie bent down, picking it up and tossing it to the side as she took a step up onto the curb. From behind her, someone grabbed her arm. Her other arm reached up instinctively to tear off her headphones and she turned to face her captor.

"Ben!" she cried out, her heart pounding. "You scared me."

He let go of her arm. "Sorry. I called your name a few times, but you must've really been into the song."

She didn't tell him that nothing had even been playing. "What are you doing here?" she asked.

He rubbed the back of his neck, looking uncomfortable. "I've been thinking, and I..." He looked defeated. She frowned, knowing it was because of her. Why couldn't she just get her shit together? "I wanted you to know that I'm in no hurry. I like you, Jo. As if that's not completely obvious. I don't think I've ever liked anyone so much. But I'm not about to push you into something you're not ready for, either."

Josie's heart would not stop pounding. It sounded like thunder in her ears.

"But I also need to know if there's hope," he continued. "That someday you might be ready?"

"I don't know, Ben," she said. Finally, she added, "I like you, too."

"What's the problem, then?"

Josie shifted her weight, wondering what to say. How could she explain her fears to him? That she found it so difficult to put her trust in the hands of someone else?

She looked up and met his eyes, feeling the confusion and pain that hung in the air between them. "I don't want to lose you," she said.

His shoulders relaxed, and he took a step toward her. "But you won't, Jo."

She wanted to pull him to her in that moment, but her arms wouldn't move.

He put a finger under her chin, lifting it so she couldn't look away. "You just have to let me in." His voice was sweet as honey. His words rich and satisfying as they slowly rolled off his tongue.

"I want to..." she began, but she didn't have time to finish. He bent down and kissed her softly.

"I want you to, too," he said.

And then he was gone.

13.

A bird never flew with one wing.

— *Danish Proverb*

JOSIE SAT UP IN BED, HER FACE DRENCHED IN SWEAT. THE wind was howling outside her window, but she barely heard it. Her heart was pounding so loudly, she thought it might leap from her chest. Slowly, she pulled back the covers, swinging her legs out and letting them hang a few inches from the floor.

The neon light from her clock was glaring. 4:15. Too early to get up, but now that she was so wide awake, she didn't think she'd be able to fall back asleep.

She pulled out her phone. Maybe Mia was awake. *R u up?* she typed.

A few seconds later her phone buzzed in her hand. *Sure am.*

She dialed quickly and waited for Mia to pick up.

"Hey," Josie whispered into the phone, realizing how silly that was when there was no one else in her apartment.

"Hey, Jo. What's up?"

"I had a bad dream. I figured you might be up, too." She pulled the comforter up around her. Even during the summer, Josie liked the feel of it around her. She slid in, tucking it around her as if she were a burrito.

"I've developed a bit of insomnia since Josef was born, which is strange since he's not here with me."

"Your body is preparing you for when he comes home and keeps you up all hours of the night."

"You know, I know people dread it, but I would give anything to experience that right now."

"I know, Mia." Josie felt the ache in her friend's voice. "You will."

"So what was your dream about?" Mia asked, keeping her voice low.

"It was strange. I was young in it—maybe three. And I was lying in bed with my mother. I had asked her to sleep with me for a little bit. I always did that. We were singing "Twinkle, Twinkle Little Star" together. Anyway, it was very dark in the room, and very cold. I kept trying to pull the comforter up, but she kept pulling it down. This went on for a long time. Well, you know how dreams are. It seemed like a long time, anyway. Finally, she ripped the blanket off the bed. I started shaking and crying. She started to move out of the room with the blanket. I tried to follow her but the floor started to swallow the bed. It was like I was sinking. My mother watched me from the hallway. She put the blanket around her. She was all wrapped up, and I was crying that the floor was going to eat me up. Suddenly, she put the blanket over her head and disappeared, right before I was going to be swallowed up by the floor."

"Then, I was suddenly in a big meadow. It was summer and I could feel the sun shining down on my face. I wasn't crying anymore, but instead I was very calm. There was a big tree nearby, and I walked over to it, ready to sit down underneath, when her face appeared in the bark and the branches became her arms. She grabbed me and started screaming, like a hawk—it was very shrill. Then I woke up."

"Geez, Jo. That's pretty intense."

"It was, yeah."

"What do you think it means?"

"I have no idea. I haven't had dreams about my mother since right after she left."

"I remember." Mia knew all too well the sleepless nights she'd had. After that day, Mia had become Josie's keeper in a way. She had started sleeping over at the Shonings' a lot in those days. "Do you think about her very often?"

"Just as much as I always have, you know. Wondering where she is. What she's doing. Why she left. It's more just because I don't know. It's hard to really care about someone when they don't really care about you."

"Sure," Mia said, yawning.

"I'm sorry, I should let you go. It's super early."

"No, it's fine, really. I nap during the day in between visits to the hospital, although I don't know what I'm going to do next week when I have to go back to work."

"Wow, already?"

"Well, I want to save some of my maternity leave for when Josef actually comes home, so yeah, I'm going to do some half days and ease back into it first, then I'll go to work and head to the hospital on my lunch break and right after work I'll meet James there."

Josie suddenly felt silly for her late-night phone call about nothing. Mia was going through something so incredibly difficult, and here she was bent out of shape about a dream.

"I'm glad you called me. Sometimes, I forget that you went through that, Jo—that you still deal with what happened. How could you not?"

"Yeah, but it happened a long time ago."

"That's true, but..." Mia paused, as if it hurt her to say it. "She was your mother."

That was one thing about Mia. Josie could always count on her to be absolutely understanding, putting into words the way Josie felt before Josie even knew she felt that way. How many times did Josie feel like she was wallowing in her circumstances? She knew she had to get past it, and she thought she did a fairly good job of putting her past where it belonged—in the past. Yet, recently she felt more affected by her mother's abandonment than ever.

"What do *you* remember about her?" Josie asked.

"Honestly, not a lot. She was never around much when we were together." Josie heard the sound of gulping, followed by a deep breath as if Mia had just taken a big drink of something. "I do remember one time, though, we were sitting on the front porch steps, and you'd been digging around in the mud, looking for worms or something. You were filthy dirty. I think I even told you you'd get walloped when your parents saw you. Anyway, your mom came outside and looked down at us. She stared at you for what seemed like hours. I was bracing for her to start carrying on. You didn't even know she was there. I watched her watching you, and then she just turned and went back inside. She didn't tell you to stop. She didn't say anything to you. She didn't say anything to me, and I was staring at her for god sakes."

"I don't think she loved me the way most moms love their children. I mean, I think maybe she did in her own way, at least at the beginning. I don't know."

"It's probably best that she left. To be so indifferent—that's what it was. She was indifferent to everything. I can't imagine being that way with Josef."

Maybe that's what was causing her to dream about her mother again. Her relationships were moving from surface-level to deeper, more intimate ones. Would she finally open up to Ben when she was scared out of her mind to do so? Would she keep being there for Payton in the midst of his mother's return? A big part of her wanted to run in the other direction, but she was growing more comfortable with her newfound ability to be immersed in what she was feeling, letting it fill her up and become part of who she wanted to be. It made her think of Louis, telling her she had some work to do. Was she finally doing it? Since she'd returned home, things had changed. Payton's mom was back. Things with Ben were as confusing as ever. But somewhere in there she had started to see her life turning out

THE BLUE JAY

the way she'd always hoped. She was finally living it, finally a participant and not just a spectator.

"I think I've always been afraid to turn out like her," Josie whispered into the phone. She'd never said it aloud before, but she realized it was the truth. Her truth, and probably what had, in so many ways, kept her standing still for so long.

"No, Jo." It wasn't sympathetic, Mia's tone. It was demanding and unwavering, like an officer barking orders to his men. "You are nothing like her."

Josie bent down over the paper, thinking. While she'd been back from Colorado for weeks, she hadn't made time to write Louis, but now, the night before the race, she felt compelled to do so. He was always lingering on the edges of her thoughts, and while guilt was as good a reason as any to sit down and write him, it was another emotion that pushed her to finally pick up her pen and begin to write.

Dearest Louis,

Since I haven't see you in almost three months, I must first ask: Are you in remission? This has been weighing on my mind greatly, and I have been hoping for good news for both you and your family.

The last time we spoke you told me I should run at life with open arms and grab onto everything I loved that I could and not let go unless I had to. I just wanted you to know I have—and I will. Not just with Ben, but with everyone. Payton, who has, in some ways, had to grow up faster than he should have had to. He's lost loved ones, he's forgiven them, he's becoming an honorable young man, and one I'm proud to know. With my dad, who continues to be my rock, even now as he begins his own journey. And while it seems impossible for me to become any closer to Mia, my surrogate mother, my best friend. I find that even she has surprised me as she becomes the kind of mother to Josef that I hope someday to be to my own kids.

MICHELLE SCHLICHER

Why is it that I'm only finally able to open myself to their love? Is it the evolving relationship with Payton that made it possible? Maybe. My guess is, though, that it wasn't until now that I was ready to. And I think I have you to thank for that. For opening my eyes to the possibility of what I'd be missing if I didn't. And for that I am very grateful.

I hope to hear from you, and know you are well. Take care of your lovely family, Louis, and continue to let them take care of you. After all, that's all anyone wants, isn't it?

Your friend,
Josie

The street was dark, but for a few lit lampposts. There was an energy all around them as other runners made their way from the grassy parking lot to the race start. Josie looked down at Payton, making big strides beside her. He was walking faster, and she had to pick up her pace to keep up with him.

"You ready for this?" she asked.

"You bet I am."

They moved through the crowds of people, making their way across one of the busier streets in Montpier. Josie saw Katherine up ahead, messing with a timing device of some sort. Music played nearby, and the sea of people seemed to move to the beats. The atmosphere was electric, which was what Josie loved about race day. There was so much positivity, the hunger to run fast, but to also feel good. It was infectious. For a first-year race, the turnout was a big feat, at least Josie thought so. It was a testament to the organization for sure. Among the faces in the crowd were many young kids who were probably in the program like Payton was. But Josie had been to a Mentor & Me event and knew there were many more participants in today's race than there were mentors and kids actually in the program, meaning people wanted to support their good cause or people were interested in joining. There was a race fee deduction for anyone who completed a Mentor & Me application before race day. She wondered how many of the people around them had taken advantage of the offer, committing themselves to not just one undertaking that would be complete at the finish line, but another disciplined endeavor, providing encouragement to someone in great need of it.

"Josie," she heard from behind. She whipped around and saw her dad crossing Walnut Street, the same street they had just crossed. He was wearing a red baseball cap, shorts and a lightweight jacket that had faded from the sun.

"Dad, you made it."

It was then Josie realized he wasn't alone.

"Of course I made it! I wouldn't miss this for anything." He turned, placing his hand on the small of the woman's back. "Josie, I'd like you to meet Leah Payne."

"Josie, I've heard so much about you," she said, reaching for Josie's hand. "And I'm really excited about this race. Your dad has been going on about it for a long time."

"I'm sure he has," Josie said. "I'm glad you could make it today, Leah. I'd been hoping to get to meet you one of these days."

"So, what's the goal today?" her dad asked, placing a hand on Payton's shoulder. "Just to finish or beat the bejeezus out of everyone else?"

"There's no pressure, Dad. We are doing this for fun." Josie took her ponytail out, then started brushing back stray hairs with her hand to redo it.

"Speak for yourself," Payton said. "I'm going for gold, Mr. McCray."

"Thatta boy."

They walked further down the path toward the small lake they would be looping for the race. Shady Lake was about .8 miles around, smack dab in the middle of the city, and surrounded by lush trees and beyond them, residential housing and a few businesses. Josie and Payton had only run the loop a few times, when they were just starting to train.

"Nice weather, eh?" Her dad unzipped his jacket, causing it to billow whenever the wind picked up.

"It's perfect," Josie agreed. For the beginning of September, she hadn't known what it would be like. The Midwest was notorious for its schizophrenic weather. With a late-in-the-day expected forecast of 53, the low 40 temps they were feeling right now meant that when the race started they'd be running in near-perfect conditions.

Josie checked her watch. 7:20.

"So what do we do now?" Payton asked, watching the runners around them.

"Stretch. Warm-up run. Keep moving. Let's find a spot where we can stretch out. You coming, Dad?"

"Nah. Leah and I are going to pick out a spot to watch the race from." He pointed off in another direction. "You two do your thing."

Josie nodded. "See you after."

"Cheer loud, Mr. McCray," Payton added. "I'll hear you."

"I'll be the loudest one," he said. "You won't be able to miss me."

Josie and Payton made their way to an open spot by the edge of the lake. "Let's start with some hip stretches," she said, crossing her left leg over her right. She hugged her left leg to her chest, twisting to look over her shoulder. Payton did the same. As they moved through several other stretches, Josie spotted Ben walking into the park, Sway trailing behind him. She waved in his direction, but he was looking in another and didn't see her. Once he'd moved into the crowd, she lost sight of him again.

"Let's skip," Payton said, bringing her back to the task at hand.

"Good idea," she replied, standing up alongside him. Power skipping was one of her favorite stretches, too. It was definitely a stretch that brought out the kid in her. By the time she would finish, she was in fits of laughter from the sheer fun of jumping, like she was a kid on a trampoline.

The Blue Jay

They skipped away from the start line, then headed back, skipping higher and higher with each step. By the time they stopped, they were both out of breath.

"Alright, kid," Josie said. "I need a drink, then we'll head back to the start. I'm sure we're not more than 20 minutes out now." She was right. It was 7:45, and more and more runners were making their way to the start to line up. She took a gulp from her water bottle, then placed it back in her drawstring bag.

Josie finished pinning her bib onto her shirt, then grabbed another safety pin to attach Payton's.

"Don't mess it up, now," she said, sticking the other pins in her mouth while she attached it. "I'm guessing you'll want to keep this race bib as a memento."

"Really?"

"Yeah! Your first one? I've still got my very first bib."

"When was that? 1995?"

"I was much older than you for my first road race, actually. 17. So, no, smartass. Not 1995." She playfully pushed him, knocking him into another runner passing by. "Sorry," she mouthed to the passerby, pulling Payton back over to her.

"Geesh, easy there, Jo."

"Sorry," she said, feeling bad. "So, anyway, back to my story. It was my senior year of high school I finally decided to train for a half-marathon. That was my one and only. Ever since I've kept to the 5K's."

Payton looked down at his number—2107—then pressed his hand over it, trying to flatten out the wrinkles.

"Think my shoes are broken in enough?"

"Oh yeah. Just the right amount of scuffed up-ness. Really, running shoes don't need to be broken in if they fit right. You haven't had any problems with yours, have you?"

"Nope. They feel great."

"Well, let's head to the start line," Josie said, patting Payton on the back.

Payton was on her heels as they maneuvered through the crowd.

"Sure are a lot of people," he said nervously as they found a spot.

"Yeah," Josie agreed. "See your mom yet?"

"Nope."

"I'm sure she's out there. Is she a good yeller?"

"She's not really the type to raise her voice, but then I've never competed in anything before."

"I'll keep an eye out for her, too." Josie wanted to be positive about Nicole. It'd taken guts to face the woman who had picked up the slack when she'd abandoned ship, and as much as Josie hated to admit, to come back to Payton and accept whatever punishment he chose to dole out to her for leaving, well that took guts, too. Luckily for Nicole, Payton wasn't one to hold a grudge.

"Okay, folks, we're about to get started," she heard Katherine say through the megaphone. "But, first we want to thank you all for supporting My Mentor & Me by coming out this morning. This is our first-ever run for the program and it's been a whopping success. All the proceeds will go to our group activities and other special events throughout the year, including our Christmas party. So, again, thank you." There were a few whoops and hollers around them before she began talking again. "Now, I'm going to hand things over to Oliver to send you off."

"Good morning!" Oliver yelled into the megaphone. He was pumped, and you could hear the exhilaration in his voice. "Is this a perfect day or what? As Katherine said, we are so excited about the turnout for today's run that we're pretty sure this won't be the only Miles for Mentors 5K we do." That prompted even more hollering. "Well, what are we waiting for?" he asked, looking to Katherine, who handed him the starting pistol.

"Here we go," Josie said to Payton. He grinned just as they heard the shot, and then they were both off and running.

The Blue Jay

For the first time since the gun sounded, Josie looked over at Payton. He'd begun striding out, and they were running in close tandem with each other.

"Feeling good?" Josie asked as she took a deep breath.

Payton used his shirt to wipe a drop of sweat from his face, then turned to Josie. "Yeah."

They were surrounded by other runners, their sneakers all hitting the pavement as they pushed forward. Their bright spandex tops, their neon running shoes glimmering in the midst of the fall colors of the landscape around them.

Josie couldn't believe this day was finally here. How long had they been training for this? She and Payton had built their friendship on the streets surrounding the Griers' house and the trails meandering through the city. Running had brought them together, and now in another mile she was going to watch him cross the finish line of his very first road race.

"Way to go, Payton! Great job!" She looked over and saw her dad and Leah cheering. Payton waved, his smile growing wider by the second.

"Just under a mile to go," she said, feeling her legs strong beneath her. While she had run many races before, she wasn't running this one for herself, and it felt good. This was Payton's day. His accomplishment. She was just happy to be part of it.

They ran further, moving around the lake, the sun glaring off the water. When they rounded the last turn to the straightaway to the finish, Payton moved beside her. His hand flew out in front of him, pointing. "Look, Josie. It's my mom!"

She turned to see Nicole, standing under a tree—its leaves a bright gold color. His mom was cheering, too, her voice loud over the other spectators. Josie waved to her as they went past, while Payton's smile, if it was even possible, grew even bigger.

"Let's finish this, shall we?" Payton nodded and they sped up, using the last of their energy to sprint to the end.

When they turned out of the chute, Nicole was waiting for them.

"That was amazing," she said. Payton ran to her, letting her hug him tightly. Nicole hugged him back, not caring about the sweat pouring off him.

"You came!" Payton said as he let go of his mom.

"I switched shifts with Dionne. I wasn't going to miss this." Nicole had found a job at the front desk of one of the larger Montpier medical clinics. The only catch was that she had to put in her time on the weekends.

"Wowie!" they heard behind them. "That sure was something!"

"Dad!" Josie said, turning to him and quickly introducing everyone. "Dad, this is Nicole, Payton's mom. Nicole, this is my dad, John McCray, and this is Leah Payne."

"It's very nice to meet you, Nicole." He extended his hand to hers, shaking it firmly. "You have quite a son, here."

"Thank you," she said, her smile almost as wide as Payton's now. There was a nice breeze coming off the water of the lake, and Josie closed her eyes, letting her body cool down from the race. Then, she opened her eyes again, scanning the crowd for Ben and Sway.

"Payton, my man." Again, from behind her. She whipped around just as Ben made his way in between them, putting an arm around Payton's shoulder.

"Ben!" Payton's face lit up. "I didn't know you were coming."

"Of course," Ben said, high-fiving him. "Wish I could've run with you, but I'm a little out of shape these days."

"Ah, you could've done it."

"Maybe if I'd pulled him along behind me," Sway added, joining in the conversation.

Josie snickered, feeling light and refreshingly happy.

14.

"Dad?" Josie called out as she entered the house. "You here?"

"I'm here!" He said from the kitchen. "Stay there. I'll be right out. We can sit on the porch for a bit."

Josie turned around, letting the screen door slam as she sat down on the front steps. She looked up, feeling a shiver of the past surround her as she scanned her surroundings. She'd sat on these steps many times as a child, drawing chalk families, blowing bubbles with Mia. Her mother would pass by, occasionally patting her small head of curls. She would look up and smile. Sometimes her mother would smile back, but usually not.

"Here we go," John said, fumbling with the latch on the screen door and pushing it out of the way, while juggling two cups of hot coffee. "Figured we'd want these this morning."

"You figured right," Josie said.

John sat down beside her. "So...the race was a success."

She smiled. "It was. Better than I had hoped. I'm so glad Nicole was able to make it."

Her father took a sip of his drink, then pursed his lips together. They sat in silence, sipping from their cups. Out of the corner of her eye, Josie saw a flash of blue and turned her head.

Pointing, she said, "Look there."

John smiled. "That mama jay has been around a lot recently. She had a nest over there earlier this year..."

"She's beautiful," Josie said under her breath, watching as the bird swooped down low to the ground and up again, disappearing into the branches of the old oak.

"Wasn't so beautiful when she thought I was coming after her nest," John said, his eyes on the spot the bird had disappeared to. "Fiercely protective they are with their young."

Thoughtful, Josie set her cup down beside her, letting it cool. "I'm nervous for him, Dad. I don't want him to get hurt."

"Of course not..." He put an arm around her shoulders and she rested her head on his. "Jo, I want to ask you something..." She felt him take a deep breath and she arched her neck so she could see him. "Do you want her to come back?"

"I used to. All the time. Every day I'd wish for her to come home." She sighed and reached for her cup again, wrapping her fingers around the handle. She took a drink. "I don't think I do anymore."

"Why do you think that is?"

"Maybe it's just been too long. I don't know her anymore. Maybe..." Josie paused, thinking. "Maybe I never really knew her. I mean, deep down. Maybe it's too late now for a second chance."

He folded his hand over hers, then pulled her to him again. "I hope she does come back," he said, finally. "I hope, someday, you're given the chance to make that decision."

"Why?"

John turned, reaching up to place his hand on her cheek. "Because I think you might choose differently than what you say. And if she's stayed away because she's afraid to face you, then it's a great disservice to you both."

Josie thought about this. Would she choose to do what Payton had and forgive? It seemed too great a thing to ask.

"You can't let pride get in the way of your own happiness. If she comes back, just lay it all out there. Ask her to do the same."

"Why are you telling me all of this?" she asked.

The Blue Jay

"Because, Jo, if someday I'm gone and not here when it happens, I want you to know what I think." He squeezed her tighter. "I'm not getting any younger, you know."

She hugged him back and closed her eyes. "I love you, Dad."

He kissed the top of her head. Josie knew he was right, and that if the day came that she saw her mother again, she would know what to do.

A few weeks later Josie received a letter in the mail. She knew it was from Louis before she even opened it. The paper was thin, and the black ink was blotted in some parts, but the handwriting was beautiful, and Josie imagined that Kass had probably fallen in love with that as much as the content.

> *Dear Josie,*
>
> *I am in remission, and let me tell you it is better news than when I found out that my sweet Kass was going to marry me—if only because now I know I've got at least a little bit more time with her here on this Earth.*
>
> *While I'd love to take credit for you giving that Ben a smidge of a chance with you, or any of the others for that matter, I can't. That falls on you, and finally letting go of the very wrong perception that one person leaving you could mean there is absolutely anything wrong with you. There's not. There never was.*
>
> *Now it's my turn to thank you, Josie. For visiting me in some of my darkest hours. You may not have realized just how afraid I was in Colorado. Facing a fight with your own mortality will shake you up more than I care to remember as I sit here on my front porch watching the sun go down, listening to Kass sing to herself as she moves around the house inside. This letter isn't sufficient, as my gratitude for the girl on the plane who kept an old man's mind from wandering to dark places is limitless. In the midst of your own peril, you were gracious and kind. The finest companion a stranger could ask for.*

Your friend,
Louis

She folded up the letter, Louis' words floating around her mind. She could picture him writing it, breathing in his surroundings and putting effort into each word. She knew she needed to get going—she was supposed to meet Ben and Payton for ice cream and she was already running late, but her emotions were running high, consuming her.

Josie walked to the window and pulled the cord to open the blinds and let the sun in. It hit her face, making her squint as she looked out over the open field across the parking lot of her apartment complex. By this time next year there would probably be two or three more buildings there. Montpier was growing every day, adding new residential neighborhoods, along with restaurants and shops that were changing the landscape of this place she called home. It was growing so fast that sometimes she barely recognized it as the "big city" she'd visited as a young girl.

On the coffee table beside her she heard her phone vibrate. Picking it up, she unlocked the screen. *At Payton's. Where r u*, it read. Quickly, she typed *On my way*, before putting the phone in her back pocket and heading for the door.

Yep, everything was changing, it seemed. She flipped off the lights, grabbed her keys and locked the door. She smiled to herself, glad to finally feel like part of the moving world she saw all around her, and for the first time, looking forward to the future, putting all her fears to rest, running full-blast into whatever might be waiting for her.

Epilogue

Josie leaned back, pushing all her weight onto the enormous oak tree behind her, and stared out at the yard. Payton was showing his mom the feeder Josie had made, while Nicole softly patted the hair on the top of his head. Mia was explaining something to Mr. and Mrs. Grier, waving her arms wildly as she spoke, while somehow still managing to hold Josef. Her father stabbed at the meat on the grill, turning it over to cook the undersides. And Ben. Ben looked up from the conversation he was having with Oliver and Katherine from the deck long enough to give her a quick smile.

There are days that will always be etched into your memory. For Josie, this day was one of them. Life felt perfect. She wanted this snapshot playing back in her head when she was ninety. She wanted to remember it always, keeping it with her like a soft blanket that a child sleeps with every night, taking it to school in his backpack for security and putting it in his pillow for sleepovers when he was far, far too old for such things. If she filled her mind with memories like this, there wouldn't be room for any other kind. And, that's what she wanted more than anything—to relieve herself of the painful remembering.

Because on that fateful winter day—her skin cold as ice, and her teeth beginning to chatter—she'd watched a dingy car pull away from the curb—from her—and plant a memory so hurtful, she felt a sense of panic each time she remembered. She had stood there, unable to move, willing her mother to turn and look one last time. But she never did. In that moment, she hadn't known if it was real. The beautiful morning she'd woken up to had gone from a dreamland to an awful nightmare in an instant, and it had been too much for a naive eight-year-old girl to process. She'd made her way back into the house, discarding her boots and hat, then climbed up the stairs to her dad, tears streaming down her face.

That was a memory that she wished to forget. How many times had she heard those words? *I'm not coming back.* She'd said them to herself over and over, always ending up asking the same question. Why? No one could answer it for her, and maybe she wasn't meant to know. Her mother most likely wouldn't have been able to even if she had been there to ask. Because the why was never worth knowing. Not if knowing it wouldn't have changed anything.

Somehow she'd gotten from there to here. Did she owe it to her dad? To Mia? To Louis? Or, maybe even Ben? Surely, it was all of them, and countless others who had helped her along the way. But on this day, her gratitude was to Payton. He'd been the one to finally make her see that all along, she'd been waiting for an answer to a question that wasn't worth knowing.

How had he done it? Taught her so much, when she was the one that was supposed to be teaching him? In just a few months, Payton had opened her heart, taught her to forgive—and to live. But most of all, he'd taught her not to be afraid.

"Hey Jo," Mia called to her. "Your turn to hold Josef."

Her friend waved her over, and Josie took the little boy into her arms, cradling his head in the crook of her elbow and stroking a finger down his cheek. They had waited to bring him home after all, not wanting to make him travel over the winter, and now that it was middle of spring, Josef was no longer an infant. At 10 months old, he had caught up to the other kids his age. He was close to walking, and probably would be if anyone would put him down long enough for him to try. They'd passed him around over and over since Mia and James had arrived with him. It was as if it wasn't enough just to see him. They needed to feel him in their arms, and know for sure that he was real. That he had finally arrived.

"Hey, little fella," she said, walking with him back toward the old oak to sit in the shade. "You and I are going to be great friends someday." Josef's piercing blue eyes looked up at her as she spoke, and one of his hands came out of the blanket that someone had tucked around him. She took it in her hand and kissed it softly. His head went up and down, resting momentarily on her shoulder, and she knew he was getting sleepy.

Finally, he nestled down against her arm, so Josie rocked him back and forth, humming so softly, she wasn't entirely sure he could even hear her. It was only a few seconds before Josef was sound asleep. She felt him relax, and the full weight of his body limp against hers.

"He's asleep," she heard behind her. Payton's voice was soft, and he knelt beside her, studying Josef.

"This is my favorite," Josie whispered back, rubbing the small of Josef's back. "They're so innocent, so perfect."

Payton ran his hand over Josef's head. "Do you think he realizes how good he's got it?" he asked, finally.

Josie looked up, moving her free hand from Josef to Payton, patting his arm.

"He will."

"You're going to be a great mom someday, Josie," he said.

The words surprised her.

"What makes you say that?"

He shrugged. "Because you stepped in as one for me. And you didn't have to do that."

She smiled, wanting to hug him in that moment.

"That means a lot to me, Payton." She glanced back down at Josef, who was sleeping soundly. "More than you know."

Payton leaned back onto the oak, the sun radiating off the top of his head, his red hair almost sparkling. "I know."

Later that afternoon after people had started to head home, Payton bounded up the steps of the deck, with a feeder in his hands.

"It's nothing special," he said, handing it to Josie's dad. "Just something my mom and I found at that antique place you like."

Her dad smiled, and Josie knew he was touched by the gift.

"I'll be back next year to clean it out for spring cleaning," he added. "That is, if Josie invites me again."

"I invited you again this year, didn't I?" Josie shot back, grinning. "Besides, you've helped two years in a row. Now you'll never get out of it."

Josie's dad held the feeder up, inspecting it. "Payton, my boy, this is quite a gift. Very thoughtful." Then, he turned to Payton, whose eyes were dancing, almost as if he was waiting for John McCray's next words. "Well, you're surely part of the family now."

The End

ACKNOWLEDGEMENTS

When I set out to write this novel, I wasn't sure I would finish it. I didn't know where it would go or how it would end. Thankfully, it went somewhere pretty special. These characters have stayed with me even as I moved on to new stories. It doesn't take much to be a mentor. It just takes being a friend. Everyone deserves a chance to be heard, to be seen, to matter. That's what mentoring is about.

There are so many people to thank for making this dream possible. I am forever grateful to each one. Justin Schlicher, husband, teacher, coach and devoted daddy. Thank you for letting me get lost in these imaginary worlds of mine for a while, for knowing me better than I know myself and for showing me time and time again what it means to truly love someone.

Trisha D., you have touched my life more than you know. I am here for you always. Grace M., you are beautiful inside and out. I can't wait to see what the future has in store for you. Hanna Piepel, you have created a stunning work of art. This cover is simply gorgeous. I am so lucky to have such a gifted friend. Elizabeth Keest Sedrel, your knowledge and advice helped turn this book into the best it could be and for that I am so grateful. Ashley Lappe, Jacquelyn Duke, Julia McFarland Mason—Thank you for your unwavering support, your diligent eyes, your infinite (and much appreciated!) advice and (most importantly) our essential (to my happiness) coffee dates, playdates and more. To all of the others who lent their talents and/or kept me sane throughout this process: Guido Henkel, Kelli Enos, Jessica Van Sloten, Kyndi Jensen, Kelly Butler, Jan Meyers, Rachel Starr, Andrea Thatcher Olson, Megan Kasperbauer, Amanda Throldahl, the Gustasons, the Livermore/Bonewitz families, the Schlichers and the Hartjes. I could not have completed this project without you. Mike Gee, we've come a long way—and I'm proud of that.

The Blue Jay

I owe a great deal to all those involved with Mentor Iowa, an organization that is changing lives with every match. Thank you to Marty Lester, Melissa Hemesath, Kristen Gruntorad and Zannie Thomas-Peckumn, as well as the countless mentors giving of their time and talents.

Terry Gustason, my loving and beautiful grandmother. You inspired me so much I created a character after you! Thank you for giving me the best gift of all—an eternal love of books. It has made this life so much richer. Jamie Gee, little sister and light of my life. Like Josie and Payton, you always strive to see the best in people. You've taught me so much by just being you. Here's to many more years of quoting D-list movies, texting each other ridiculously hilarious memes (in our eyes at least) and eating way too many snacks. Joni and Ron Livermore, my biggest supporters. I love you. Thank you for always believing I had it in me. And to Sawyer and Sullivan Schlicher, my sweet girls. You are everything.

About the Author

Michelle Schlicher lives in Iowa with her family. This is her first novel.

www.michelleschlicher.com

Facebook.com/michelleschlicherbooks

Follow @chelleschlicher

Made in the USA
Middletown, DE
13 April 2016